The Redacted Sherlock Holmes Volume VII

By

Orlando Pearson

Paperback ISBN 978-1-80424-002-1
ePub ISBN 978-1-80424-003-8
PDF ISBN 978-1-80424-004-5

Published by MX Publishing
335 Princess Park Manor, Royal Drive,
London, N11 3GX
www.mxpublishing.co.uk

Cover design Jane Dixon-Smith

Contents

Foreword

Followers of *The Redacted Sherlock Holmes* series have often asked how many of the historical events retold in the collections published to date actually happened as described. So, taking examples from each volume backwards from VI to I:

- Was there a French female composer called Augusta Holmès who was Sherlock Holmes's sister?

- Did Winston Churchill seek Holmes's help at the height of the Battle of Britain and of the Blitz, and was the bombing of neutral Ireland by the Germans in 1941 one of the results of this consultation?

- Was the 1930s German tennis star, Gottfried von Cramm, Sherlock Holmes's grandson, and was von Cramm's redoubtable mother the result of a liaison between Holmes and Irene Adler?

- Was the winter of 1894/5 one of such monstrous ferocity that Holmes was asked to investigate whether 19th century industrialisation was causing changes in the climate?

- Did the Prince of Wales, Albert Edward, later King Edward VII, plot to usurp Queen Victoria as monarch, and did Sherlock Holmes make a discovery that thwarted this?

- Was Holmes engaged by the British government in 1945 to assess whether Hitler's deputy, Rudolph Hess, was fit to stand trial at Nuremburg?

Followers of the series who look up for themselves more details about the events referred to in the thirty-seven works (thirty-six short and one long) published to date, will find that the series presents the matters covered in a way that is consistent with the known facts. The redaction of the involvement of Sherlock Holmes was generally made on grounds of national security or because the matters Holmes uncovered were too shocking for them to be made public knowledge. It is to be rejoiced that the publication of these accounts of historic events withheld by Dr Watson allow the record to be set straight, and that the role of Sherlock Holmes at some of the key turning points in world history can finally be revealed.

Sherlock Holmes's dealings with famous people was the inspiration for the front covers of the books. It is not spoiling the plot of the works in this collection when I disclose that the people featured on the front of this book are two kings, two poets, an artist, a model, a menagerist, a Classical scholar, a diplomat, a man found guilty of high treason, a drinks manufacturer, and an accountant. Some may note that this list gives more people than the seven figures shown opposite Sherlock Holmes. The aim of this introduction is not to solve mysteries when it precedes writings about the greatest mystery-solver of all, but a reading of *The Poet and his Muse* and of *The Cherry-Tree and the Comma* will resolve the apparent anomaly.

In this volume I have decided for the first time to put a brief explanation after each work of how much of what Dr Watson retells is the history of the event as we know it, and how much is new or may have been romanticised (Holmes's words about Watson's writings) or elaborated by Watson.

I hope readers of these works find the explanation enhances their enjoyment, and I am available under the email address name OrlandoDLPearson@gmail.com to answer any questions.

Orlando Pearson

London 2022

The Poet and his Muse

"Draw your chair up, good Watson, and hand me my violin, for the only problem we have still to solve is how to while away these bleak autumnal evenings."

And with these words from Holmes, I concluded the case of *The Noble Bachelor* in which Holmes located the eponymous bachelor's missing bride and explained the reason for her disappearance immediately after her marriage to Lord St Simon in Hanover Square.

It was October 1887 and shortly before what was to be the first of my two weddings.

I confess that having seen Lord St Simon's marriage voided before my eyes – our petitioner deprived, in Holmes's slightly sardonic words, of a wife and a fortune in the space of the four hours between his arrival at our door at four-o-clock in the afternoon and the case's denouement at eight o-clock the same evening, I felt, for the first time, some misgivings about my own impending nuptial. For, as I sat at the fireside, the uncomfortable thought occurred to me, not I confess for the first time, that whatever my heart was telling me, I in fact knew very little about the fair Miss Mary Morstan.

As these uneasy thoughts flitted through my head, Holmes finished tuning his violin and put it to his chin.

When he took up his fiddle, I never knew quite what would emerge from under his fingers. Sometimes it was the most intellectually rigourous music – Bach he told me – and the counterpoint in the music seemed to reflect the logical processes of his mind. At other times, no more than the most desultory noises issued forth as though he were lost in a thought incapable of any form of articulation. And sometimes, particularly after the resolution of a difficult case, he would, perhaps in celebration, dash off the most exuberant and challenging showpieces in the instrument's repertoire – Pablo de Sarasate, whom we subsequently heard perform at St James's Hall, Nicolo Paganini, and Henryk Wieniawski.

But on this occasion what he played fitted into none of these categories. The music's technical difficulty could not be doubted for it contained double-stopping, triple-stopping, and notes right at the top end of the violin's range. But it also conveyed a sense of the welling up of emotions which could not be mistaken for anything else.

Eventually, when my friend had laid his bow to rest, I felt nothing I could say would be adequate to follow what he had just played, and it was he who broke the silence, adopting a voice quite alien to his normal, dry tones.

"As the music rises higher and higher and floods on to its magnificent climax, Isolde is swept away on the crest of the song, past the sorrowing onlookers, to join Tristan in the vast wave of the breath of the world…Night and Death and Love are one."

"Is what you have just said," I asked, and paused while I looked for the right word, "not perhaps a little grandiloquent?"

"The piece," came a faraway voice, "was my own version for solo violin of the *Liebestod* or *Lovedeath* from *Tristan and Isolde* by Richard Wagner. And the words I have just spoken are what the composer himself said about it. Do you not feel that those words capture the passion of the music and of love which in Wagner's great opera is entwined with death?"

In all the years I had shared quarters with Holmes at Baker Street, we had never spoken of such personal and delicate matters. It had never been my desire to force a confidence, but I did feel as we sat on either side of the hearth on that October evening, that Holmes had something of great personal significance that he wanted to impart. But I was not sure how to ask him to do so without running the risk of sounding inquisitive and in so doing do causing him to clam up.

"Is what you have just called a *Liebestod* or Lovedeath something you yourself have experienced," I said at last – and I paused before I selected my next words with studied ambiguity – "in practice?"

I still would not have been at all surprised if Holmes had either not answered, or if he had rebuffed me. In the end I was quite relieved when he leant back in his chair, and said in a non-committal tone, "Love and death have been intertwined in literature through the ages. *Tristan and Isolde* – that was Wagner's take on it but the story of that name dates back to at least the Middle Ages. *Pyramus and Thisbe* is from Ovid though far more ancient than the two thousand years old version that has come down to us, while *Romeo and Juliet* is a Shakespearean version of a much older story from Italy. *The Sufferings of Werther* is a work which Goethe bases on real events – just, good Watson, like your chronicles of my activities."

At this reference to his own activities, I thought Holmes might now revert to his normal ascetic self, but his next words showed that his thoughts were taking him in another direction.

"Old Goethe even gives his hero a name which means 'worthier' as though to endorse the actions of his tragic hero who kills himself as his love is unrequited."

My initial impression of Holmes's knowledge of literature had been that it was nugatory. But over the years of our acquaintance, he had quoted Goethe and Flaubert in the original as well as Hafeez in translation. My impression of Holmes's intellect had thus been somewhat modified, but I still felt bound to commend him on the commanding sweep of his reading. I was about to do so when I noted from the deep red glow of the tobacco in the bowl of his pipe, that his mood had taken him from the feelingless being that I have so often characterised him as, into something altogether different.

"I do not think," he added when he spoke again, this time in a very uncertain voice, as though not even sure whether I would want to listen to him, "that I have ever told you of my very first case."

I had always wanted to know what had started my friend on his career as a detective – I had assumed there would be some tale of derring-do at a boarding school, and I was not sure whether his latest remark was a prelude to him returning to his normal mode – and so I held my counsel.

But Holmes seemed uncharacteristically eager to expand and he continued, "As you will see, it ended with me uncovering a matter of the greatest interest, yet my handling of the case was wrong in every sense. But there is no case from which I learnt so much, and it was after the case's conclusion I resolved to adopt the career I have chosen."

What I write now is what Holmes told me on that October night of 1887.

Holmes paused before he continued to speak and then played a few notes on the violin as though to clear his throat.

" 'Poète, prends ton luth; le vin de la jeunesse fermente cette nuit dans les veines,' " he quoted. At my look of puzzlement, he translated, " 'Poet, take up thy lute, the wine of youth is this night rising to its peak in the veins.' "

And with this entirely uncharacteristic dash of poetry, Holmes commenced his narrative.

> It is hard indeed, not be borne away on romance when quoting a poet in a Romance language. But it was an Italianate rather than a French poet who provided me with that first case. Before I embark on this narrative, I must insist that if you produce a version of what I am about to tell you tonight, you will have to ensure it does not appear in our lifetimes. I would not wish my public

to know that there is anything to me beyond the logical machine you portray me as, or what caused me to hide my emotional life behind the rational façade of your portrayal. Even at the age of thirty-three, a man must think of how he will be seen by posterity.

I nodded my assent to the request but only spoke to ask, "So your first case was in Italy?"

Alas, no, although, as you will learn, there is an Italianate element to it.

By the time I was five, both my parents had died, so I spent my formative years being passed around between their relatives and associates – as is the fate of orphaned children the world over.

By and large, I think I was treated well by the people with whom I lodged, and in the autumn of 1869 – so, eighteen years ago – I found myself, at the house of a distant cousin of my mother, the Verners, in their Thameside house at number 15 Cheyne Walk in Chelsea. I had been here before, though when or how I cannot now tell, and Verner was the anglicised name of Vernet, the French artist, from whom my mother was descended.

In the years since 1869, the Thames has been embanked and the houses at Chelsea now stand back from the river but, at the time of which I now tell, the only thing that separated the rather splendid abode from the course of the river was the grass of their front gardens before the door and a narrow, mirey road to bring up horses and carriages. Henry VIII had had a manor-house in the area and in the gardens behind the row of houses in which my mother's cousins lived, there were traces of it, as well as of ancient mulberry trees that are supposed to have been planted by Elizabeth I, and which I had shinned up in previous visits to Chelsea.

The Thames is heavily tidal in Chelsea so at high-tide it sometimes lapped only a few yards from the house while at low-tide its shrunken flow was flanked by broad, grey, and not always sweet-smelling mudflats.

On my first night at this stay at Cheyne Walk, I was woken just before dawn by a curious noise.

It was a high-pitched cry from outside the front of the house.

It did not sound to me to be human but of course the fact that I did not think the sound was human did not tell me what the cry actually was. And as a naïve fifteen-year-old, nothing occurred to me. You will appreciate that even as recently as 1869 London was entirely without any form of lighting and so, hard though I stared out into the darkness, I could not discern what its source might be.

There it was again! A high-pitched squeal.

Holmes put his violin to his chin once more, and he stroked his bow across its strings with his fingers all but on the violin's bridge. A distinctly unmusical sound was emitted – although I can attest that such unmusical sounds were not so unusual when my friend extemporised.

Even at so young an age (Holmes continued) I found schoolwork facile and was aware that I was endowed with exceptional investigative powers. Accordingly, I resolved to investigate the source of the noise as soon as it got light on that Saturday morning.

The mudflats on the morn – the page unlocked the front doors of the house, as soon as dawn turned the night sky grey, and I was out on them as soon as he had done so – bore the marks of footprints. And they were not the webbed prints of an aquatic bird such as a swan or a goose – but of what looked like a large biped with three pointed toes plus a rear spur. And beside it the footprints of a man of medium build. And everywhere the three-toed biped had left its traces, the human footprints were to be seen beside it. I could only assume it had been kept on a leash by the man.

At this point I had not really considered a career path for myself and accordingly I had not yet elevated the practice of tracing and following footprints to being the subject of a monograph. Nevertheless, even at this young age I was sufficiently astute to follow both the human and the non-human footprints to the front door of the house at number 16.

So who lived there and what animal did he keep?

I went into breakfast and, as I sat over my porridge, I resolved to follow our neighbour at the first opportunity.

This was not long in coming.

My subsequent tracking of our neighbour was greatly helped by the expansion of the London train and Underground network. Before 1863, there was no London Underground and following someone of the social status of the person who lived next door to the Verners at Cheyne Walk would have required a horse. As it was, the clock had not struck ten on the same morning when I saw from my window the Verners' neighbour, with a neatly-trimmed red beard and dressed in black from top-hat to boots, head off from number 16.

I followed him on foot for twenty minutes to what turned out to be South Kensington Station which had then only been open for a year. My parents had left me with a reasonable allowance, so I was able to pay for a ticket for the train, and off we went. Your readers may see some significance in the fact that that on this, my first case, the station at which my quarry descended from the train was Baker Street, but this was not a matter over which I had any control.

From Baker Street, he walked east along the Marylebone Road, turned left into Regent's Park, and walked across it to arrive at the southern entrance of London Zoo.

I followed him through the turnstile and then watched him as he strode purposefully through the zoo and ended up by the cage of an animal I had never heard of before – the wombat. This is a short-legged roan mammal from Australia about three feet in length and with a disproportionally large head. A plaque at the side of the cage described the enclosure as the Wombat's Lair and told of the animal's habits which included carrying its young in a pouch and burrowing at will.

I walked round to the other side of the cage and observed my neighbour as he stared into the cage with a look of what I can only call supreme longing.

I then saw him take out a notebook and started to – well, from my station at the other side of the cage, I was not sure what he started to do – and I moved round so that I now stood behind him. To anyone observing me, I thought, I would look as though I were staring into the fenced enclosure, but in fact I was looking at what my neighbour was entering into his book.

He proceeded, first, to sketch the low-slung, coarse-haired beast, an activity for which he had obvious talent, and then wrote in a child-like hand on the page as I looked from ten feet behind him:

Oh! How the family affections combat
Within this heart, and each hour flings a bomb at
My burning soul! Neither from owl nor from bat
Can peace be gained until I clasp my wombat.

I concluded on the meagre evidence of this verse that my neighbour was a considerably better artist than poet while, having completed his ditty, he seemed done for the day, and I followed him back to Baker Street Station, and thence to Cheyne Walk.

I trailed him at every opportunity over the next few of days and it became clear that his trip to the wombat cage at London Zoo was like a pilgrimage for he repaired there on each occasion and spent long hours doing no more than staring like an unrequited lover into the cage.

It was on Tuesday the fifth of October that the event occurred that forms the core of the matters of which I now describe.

Our neighbour paid his normal visit to the zoo, but where was it that he was heading afterwards? For he did not make to return towards Baker Street station.

Instead, he headed north and visited a plant-nursery by Lords Cricket Ground. Here he seemed to have an acquaintance for I overheard him say, "I will return them e'er the day is out." Then he headed off with a heavy-duty spade and a hefty mattock which he slung over his shoulder so that they jutted out of what we would say today was a bag for carrying golf-clubs, although such bags did not exist in 1869. This bag he slung over his shoulder.

Was he going back to the zoo to spring a wombat, I wondered – he obviously had no regular use for gardening implements or he would not have wanted to borrow some for the afternoon – or was our destination to be somewhere else?

At first as I tracked him, I assumed the Zoo was indeed his objective for his route took him east along the Regent's Canal, and I thought he would turn right into the Zoo's precincts by its northern entrance. But instead, he continued to Camden Town. There he got onto the over-ground train at Camden Road station and headed two stops north-west to Gospel Oak. Thence he turned left under the bridge that took the line over the street and then headed north across a corner of Parliament Hill Fields to end up at the entrance to Swain's Lane, a vertiginous throughfare that I knew even then ended in Highgate Village atop Highgate Hill.

But our trek ended just short of that summit, at Highgate Cemetery.

"Had he not noticed he was being followed?" I interjected.

"Even at an early age, good Watson," responded my friend, some of his customary asperity back in his voice, "seeing no one is what one should expect to see when one is followed by me. But what followed next was not what I expected to see."

My quarry (he continued) seemed to have a specific purpose to his visit.

He entered the cemetery at four o'clock, just before it closed on the west or old side as opposed to the more recent east side, and headed briskly uphill, before he took a left turn. His journey had its conclusion at a grave located at the end of a path that was obscured and over-grown.

He stood there for some little while, and then, clearly overcome, knelt before it, while I stood perhaps fifteen or twenty yards behind him although I had taken the precaution of concealing myself behind a massive and ancient oak tree.

As it was obvious that this grave was the spade-carrying occupant of number 16's planned destination, and, as I could think of no other objective for this visit equipped with digging equipment than to exhume a body, I felt obliged to watch what happened next. I decided to climb the tree – my climbing skills honed by my climbing of the ancient mulberry trees behind Cheyne Walk – until I was on an over-hanging branch directly above my neighbour's head. But with what end in mind did he want to disinter a corpse? At the sensitive age of fifteen, it boggled my mind.

"It boggles mine now nearly a score years later," I responded uneasily, for once by no means sure that I wanted to hear any more of this account of my friend's activities.

My friend continued, ignoring my interruption, and indeed, judging from his rapt features, completely immersed in the world of his narrative.

My quarry stood up as though he had heard something, and he was soon joined by a small party of other men. One, I could see from the stain of iodine on his finger, was a doctor and another, from a sheaf of papers I saw sticking out of his pocket, a lawyer.

They proceeded to light an enormous bonfire at the graveside. The damp wood crackled noisily and the acrid smoke from it smote my nostrils as I sat on my perch with such force, that it was fortunate that my lungs were already tempered by several years of tobacco smoking for otherwise I am sure I would have betrayed my presence by coughing. They then started to dig by the fire's flickering light.

After half an hour's digging, a coffin was brought to the surface.

It was only after some wrestling with a clamp which my neighbour removed from an inside pocket, that he was able to wrench open the coffin's lid.

He stood back and the body I could see beneath me was of a woman of the greatest beauty. She was quite remarkably intact – her auburn hair that lay along her back appeared to have grown to fill the coffin, and it shone like ripe corn in the waxing and waning light from the flames, while her pale, clear, delicate features were undiminished by her long sleep.

"Is an uncorrupted body not one of the prerequisites for sainthood?" I asked.

I confess the sight of the beautiful body, (continued Holmes, again ignoring me) literally unearthed after a long period buried, had the profoundest effect on me, and this effect continues to this day.

Holmes drew heavily on his pipe and this time I withheld any interjection. It was in anything other than in his normal clipped tones that the eventually resumed his narrative.

For months afterwards I saw only her face when I closed my eyes and I see her face sometimes now and it always comes between me and any softer feelings I might have.

A long pause and then a voice which seemed to come from the depths of my friend's soul.

> For I know what true beauty is. And I know that anything comparable to what I have seen will always be unattainable for me.

I left Holmes uninterrupted for some time while his normally austere features seemed to crumple before me and all I could hear was the sound of him sucking in smoke from his pipe.

In the end I felt he might now actually welcome a comment from me, and I asked in as gentle a voice as I could manage.

"So, what happened next?"

Even now there was a long pause before my friend continued his narrative.

> My neighbour replaced the lid of the coffin within the briefest time of opening it, so I had no idea of what his reason might have been to open it. He or someone in his party had apparently brought a hammer and nails for the purpose of resealing it which he did himself with considerable vigour. And two members of the party then spent some time replacing the earth that had been removed.
>
> Within another half an hour, they had extinguished the fire, and were gone.

I was too shaken to make any attempt to shadow anyone. Indeed, it was some little time before I could bring myself to descend the tree. I had to climb a wall to get out of the cemetery and, to go back to the Verners, I went down Highgate Hill and walked to Kentish Town to return to Cheyne Walk via King's Cross.

I was at a loss as to whether to tell anyone what I had seen. Who was the right authority and who would believe me in any case?

I took to my bed. I told the Verners I had a chill, and the doctors they kindly brought to see me diagnosed brain-fever and recommended four-hourly doses of brandy until I felt better.

It was about a week after the events that I described that I was lying in my bed one afternoon when I heard another strange sound.

The tide was up and there on the narrow strip of land between the houses and the river, I saw our neighbour leading a wombat on a lead.

"You had not described the cry of a wombat from your observation of the animal at the zoo."

"It is a sort of suppressed shriek, vey audible from distance," replied my friend. Putting his violin to his chin, he proceeded to play another unmusical note on his violin, this time with his fingers much lower down on the strings.

"So where had he got it?"

"When I saw him getting the digging tools from the nursery at Lord's, I had of course wondered if he had been going to spring the wombats from their London Zoo enclosure. They had been caged but their front paws were far more eloquent about their digging capabilities than the little table with information about the species. Certainly, it would only have required a little help with digging equipment to facilitate their escape. But he had said, when he picked up the tools that he would return them that day, and it would have been too late to get back into the zoo after his exhumation of the body at Highgate Cemetery."

"I am now at a loss. You were finding out the source of a high-pitched noise from what you think is a biped avian on a leash, you have followed your neighbour to the zoo where he spent long periods at the wombat cage, you have witnessed him exhume a body and then re-inter it, and now you are engaged in finding out how he has got hold of a wombat of his own. What did you do next?"

"I was not then armed with the experience of life in its fullness nor the authority that comes with age. In the end, I went to the police-station and asked if I could make a statement."

"Were they not taken aback by the matters that you described?"

"I think they were. I was sent from the police-station in Kensington, straight to Highgate Cemetery, and I went up the slope to the site of the exhumation accompanied by a somewhat sceptical young constable called Gregson. The disturbance of the soil around the grave and the blackened remains of sticks made what had happened obvious, even nearly a week after the event."

"What was the Gregson's response to your discovery?"

"He noted my observations in a methodical fashion and passed the matter to his superiors. I will spare you the tedium of listening to all the meetings and discussions that took place, but within a shorter time than you would have believed, I found myself in an office in Whitehall sitting before the solemn-looking Henry Bruce."

"The Liberal politician and former Home Secretary?"

"The same, though with his ruffed shirt and hair over his ears he looked more like a concert-pianist than a statesman. Home Secretary was his position in 1869 although he has since been elevated to the peerage. The only other person in the room was a very young, although as it turned out, very able civil servant."

Holmes rose to poke the fire before he continued his narrative.

"I am most disturbed by the accounts I have heard of your spooring, young man," started the Home Secretary, who, despite his Scottish name, hailed from

South Wales and had a lilting and not unmusical Welsh accent.

I was not sure how to deal with this opening.

"I have," I said at length, "brought to the attention of the authorities a clear case of a man desecrating a grave which is a breach of the law of the land. I have also identified a case of the same man keeping an exotic animal – a wombat – which he may or may not have obtained irregularly but the means he used to desecrate the grave would lend themselves equally well to purloining an animal from London Zoo where I have observed this person watching the wombat cage with a frequency that amounts to obsession."

"And," asked the young civil servant, "have you gone to London Zoo to check that all their wombats are still there?"

"I have not had the opportunity to do so. I have been laid low by fever since the events that I reported and which official investigations have confirmed to have taken place," I replied.

"And had you made any enquiries into the neighbour that you have been tracking?"

"I have not," I replied. "I thought that the matters I was investigating were sufficiently serious, that such investigations were superfluous."

"You are living next door to him. I would have thought that a fifteen-year-old such as yourself might initiate some discourse with the domestic staff of either your own household or that of your neighbours and so might have elicited useful information about him."

"My curiosity had been piqued by the curious noises I had heard at night, and I then dedicated my time to following my neighbour."

"I see. And have you given any thought to identifying the person whose grave he breached?"

"By the time my quarry had finished at the grave, it was too dark to read any inscription, and I did not think to investigate the identity of the person or people buried in the grave when I went there with Constable Gregson."

"You have made no attempt to investigate why your neighbour made his way to a specific grave to open it, what he did there – for you say that the opening of the coffin was for a fleeting moment – and whether it is connected with the appearance of a wombat on the foreshore at Chelsea."

"I accept all your comments on my investigation," I said eventually. "As I have said, I have been laid low with the brain-fever since I returned to Cheyne Walk from a darkened Highgate Cemetery and I have not had the opportunity since then to elucidate the points you have raised."

"Did it occur to you that the authorities at Highgate Cemetery would not allow someone to dig up a body willy-nilly."

"I had no inkling that my neighbour was going to Highgate Cemetery when I followed him."

"But surely," said the civil servant, "you knew that a lawyer and a doctor were present when you were at the cemetery. And the cemetery's proprietors showed no interest in what was happening even though, not only did your neighbour arrive with digging equipment on his shoulder, but the party also lit a large fire. Surely that was enough to enable you to exclude the possibility that this was an unsanctioned disinterment and to focus your energies on finding the ineluctable truth behind what was happening."

I was at a loss for words.

"And have you told anyone apart from the police of your findings on this matter?" interjected the Home Secretary.

"I have not."

"Well, you have at least got something right," said Home Secretary Mr Bruce with a sigh. "In the circumstances. I might as well tell you the facts behind what has happened, and we will see what we can do to make sure this does not get into the press. Your neighbour is the widowed poet and artist, Dante Gabriel Rossetti, who is a friend of mine, and whose name declares his family's Italian origin. His wife, who died after a still-born birth eight years ago, is buried in the grave."

The minister paused before continuing.

"As well as being his helpmeet, Rossetti's wife, Elizabeth Siddal, was his muse for both his poetry and for his art. With her, he had buried a hand-written copy of some unpublished poems, and without her he is bereft of poetic inspiration."

I felt it was inappropriate to comment that I could confirm this want of inspiration if the verse I had seen at the wombat cage was anything to go by.

The Home Secretary continued.

"Rossetti had told me he was pressed for money and has had an offer of an advance from a publisher if he can produce another book of verse. He felt that the easiest way to satisfy the publisher's request is to retrieve the manuscript."

"You make yourself very plain," I said.

"He prevailed upon me as a close friend and Home Secretary, to grant him a special dispensation to retrieve his poems, and this I agreed to do. I saw little purpose in issuing a downright refusal which might in any case be ignored, so instead I insisted it take place as discretely as possible – thus, at night with only the poet's own people present. I little realised what he might do with the money that he has now received."

The statesman paused again.

"As someone who has a taste for conducting private investigations, you might like to consider what an intelligent, widowed man in a well-to-do area might need money for."

"I fear," I replied, "as your colleague has already established, I do not know enough about Mr Rossetti to express an opinion. It is a capital mistake to theorize before one has data. Insensibly one begins to twist facts to suit theories, instead of theories to suit facts."

"I think", interjected the young civil servant at Mr Bruce's side, "your account of events has given you enough data to form a tenable hypothesis. As well as being a poet and an artist, Mr Rossetti is a menagerist. The bird whose cry you heard was a peacock, the Home Secretary has said Rossetti has bought himself a pair of wombats using the proceeds of the advance. One died almost immediately, but he has given the name Top to the other one and he takes it for walks along the river."

"And so, no offence has been committed?"

"Only, I fear," retorted the Home Secretary, "that of wasting police time, young man."

My friend's narrative came to an abrupt, conclusive, and not unhumorous end, but I was curious about what he had learnt from the case.

I put this to him.

"As the young civil servant said, I ought to have made some enquiries of the neighbours" – something Holmes was to do, albeit with indifferent results, in the adventure of *The Solitary Cyclist*. "And, before raising the matter with the authorities, I ought to have checked that there was actually some foul play going on. Sometimes in my cases I have feel I have caused more harm than good in my investigations," – something Holmes was to re-iterate in *The Abbey Grange* case – "and I resolved after this that I would take on a case only if specifically commissioned to do so, and I would only reveal my hand when I had full knowledge and when I thought it right so to do."

And I can attest, that in all the cases I worked on with Holmes, there was always some petitioner, be it a policeman, a politician, or a private individual, who instigated the case that Holmes in my company investigated, and that he never declared the case solved until the evidence was more than over-whelming. And, as I realised some time later, the young civil servant who was so versed in how to conduct an investigation although he had apparently made no attempt to do so himself, was none other than a twenty-two-year- old Mycroft Holmes.

"And it was looking at the peacock footprints on the shore which taught me the value of making notes on tracks of all sorts which eventually found a place in my monograph upon the tracing of footsteps, with some remarks upon the uses of plaster of Paris as a preserver of impressions."

"But you have not explained how this matter was what made you decide to make investigative work your life."

There was a long pause before Holmes rose, took the poker in his hand, added further coals to the glowing embers, and applied the bellows until the fire burst back into life.

He was still bent over the fire when he next spoke sounding very much as though he were not speaking to me at all.

"I felt no one I ever saw could eclipse the beauty of the figure I saw in that coffin in the night of the fifth of October 1869. Beauty without the beloved is like a sword through the heart and yet I cannot feel that I have suffered anything by comparison with Elizabeth Siddal's one loss, or with her double-bereaved husband. But I did not wish to become like the rather over-wrought Werther whose suicide for unrequited love was an act wholly alien to my outlook. That remains my view still."

He sat back down and, when he next spoke much of the old certainty had returned.

"By contrast my first case had shown me that I had much still that I could improve on in my investigative work. And having something where I can work to make myself worthier is a distraction from what even now I can do no other than count as a loss."

"And did you ever have an opportunity to speak to Mr Rossetti?"

I fear (replied Holmes, taking up his narrative once more) that, as is the fate of orphaned children the world over, I was soon on my way to another relative so opportunities for that were scant.

But, as I stood outside the Verners' house wating for the carriage to arrive to move me and my possession to my next address, I saw him, dressed as ever in the black of mourning, hunched in grief on the Thames foreshore, looking out over the water. I felt I had no choice but to speak to him even if only to offer to get him a glass of water.

"My wombat has died," said he, turning to me as he heard my approach.

I feigned ignorance of what he might be referring to, but he explained anyway.

"I am a poet. And my muse has deserted me. I thought the recovery of a lost manuscript," and here he plucked some holed and mildewed paper out of an inside pocket, although he forbore to tell me whence it had come, "or the ownership of a rare beast, might help me recover it. But this manuscript has not helped me and now my wombat, my last hope of inspiration, is no more."

As a fifteen-year-old youth, I was not at all sure what I should say as I did not feel it quite my place to comfort someone to whom I was a stranger, and in any case I doubted I had the words adequate for the task.

I looked out across the river in search of some spark of inspiration. It had been a wet autumn and it was flowing turbid and greyish brown before our eyes, dragging driftwood speedily downstream.

"The passage of life," I ventured at last, "is like the eddying flow of the great Thames before us. Betimes it is high tide, betimes low ebb, but even in grief, even in death, we, who for however brief a span remain spared, can dream that life may yet yield delight once more."

"And that was the extent of your discussion with him?"

"At that point, the carriage to collect me arrived and I was unable to prolong the interview."

"So was Rossetti in the end able to publish further poems?"

"Contrary to my initial impression, Rossetti was indeed a talented poet, and he did publish further collections. And in his next collection he issued a new version of his best-known poem, *Sudden Light,* which contained a completely different final verse from what it had had at its original publication."

My friend paused, and a light of joy came into his eyes before he said, "This new version draws heavily on what I said to Rossetti that day on the Thames's shore." And, rather than reaching for his archives, Holmes leant back in his chair and recited words which were obviously close to his heart:

"I have been here before,
But when or how I cannot tell:
I know the grass beyond the door,
The sweet keen smell,
The sighing sound, the lights around the shore.

You have been mine before, –
How long ago I may not know:
But just when at that swallow's soar
Your neck turn'd so,
Some veil did fall, – I knew it all of yore.

Has this been thus before?
And shall not thus time's eddying flight
Still with our lives our love restore
In death's despite,
And day and night yield one delight once more?"

"I am not sure in this instance," he concluded, "who is the poet and who the muse. But I do not believe I would have inspired the poet if I had not been myself the subject of a source of inspiration which continues to inspire me even now."

The Poet and his Muse – Afterword

The Pre-Raphaelite poet, artist, and menagerist, Dante Gabriel Rossetti, lived at Cheyne Walk in Chelsea. Cheyne Walk, with its picturesque surroundings, has always attracted creative talents – novelist George Elliot, composer Ralph Vaughan Williams, and philosopher Bertrand Russell, among many others, made their homes there. It is thus unsurprising that Sherlock Holmes's relatives, the Verners, descendants of French artist Vernet, should also have chosen it as their address, or that events there should have had such a powerful impact on the young Sherlock Holmes.

Rossetti got legal permission to exhume the body of his wife, Elizabeth Siddal, from the family vault in Highgate Cemetery in 1869. The Cemetery is open to the public and the vault of the Rossetti is still there under lofty overhanging trees although the burial place of Dante Gabriel Rossetti himself is at Birchington-on Sea in North Kent where the poet went in 1882 in an attempt to restore his failing health. A visit to Highgate Cemetery is well worth an afternoon of anyone's time.

Among the party of people in attendance at Siddal's disinterment was a friend of Rossetti called Charles Augustus Howell. He is widely thought to have been a blackmailer.

Fans of the stories of Arthur Conan Doyle may note the resemblance between the names Charles Augustus Howell and the blackmailer Charles Augustus Milverton in the Conan Doyle story of that name. Milverton and Howell both came to a violent end with the authorities at a loss as to who killed them.

As well as going to Highgate Cemetery, visitors to London can follow the rest of the routes along which the young Sherlock Holmes trailed Rossetti in 1869 although in 1906 a new station called Regent's Park was opened which is now the closest underground station to London Zoo rather than Baker Street.

Siddal is the first picture in the top row of the cover and Rossetti is next to her. She was the muse for several artists of the pre-Raphaelite movement and apart from the picture of her on the cover, the most famous representation of her is the one below by John Everett Millais entitled *Ophelia*.

A Study in Black and Orange

When I first made the acquaintance of Sherlock Holmes, I was living in a small hotel in the Strand. This rapidly proved to be beyond my pocket, and even when as a measure to save costs, I had started to share quarters in Baker Street with Holmes, my financial fortunes waxed and waned. I could spend as much as I wanted, as long as it did not exceed the eleven shillings and sixpence a day which was my army pension, and I sought to augment my income by speculations on the turf and on the stock market. While my investments in both of these gave me intermittent bursts of prosperity, there were also times when they rendered my financial situation precarious indeed.

My reader will recall that in *The Sign of Four*, I challenged my friend to make deductions on a pocket-watch that had come into my possession after the early death of my elder brother who had inherited it from our long-deceased father. Amongst more things than I would have believed possible, Holmes deduced from scratched numbers on the timepiece's casing that it had often been used as a pledge at a pawnbrokers. It is here that I must confess to my reader that now that the watch – a fifty guinea specimen, as Holmes rightly estimated – had come down to me, I used it in the same way as my brother had. I was a habitue of Dyers of Bloomsbury on the west side of Endell Street and just north of Covent Garden. Mr Dyer's shop was small and cramped but it was far enough away from Baker Street to give me the anonymity that I craved for what I regarded as a shaming act required *in extremis* when I needed to make ends meet.

Dyer would advance against a range of pledges. As well as personal jewellery like my watch, he took household equipment such as mangles and clothing. I soon learnt that pop goes the weasel was a reference to pledging a coat (or weasel and stoat in the parlance of the eastern part of London) in exchange for an advance. Because my speculative gains occurred irregularly, my visits to Mr Dyer's emporium took place with a similar lack of regularity, but their regrettable frequency enabled me to observe – I had not shared quarters for some years with Holmes for nothing! – some patterns in the pawnbroker's callers.

In the second half of the week, when working people were pressed as they waited for their weekly wage, I would stand in a queue behind the wives of labourers pawning an iron, whereas coming up to quarter days, it would be a normally be a more well to do person, who, down on his luck, and needing an advance to meet his rental, might pawn silver to obtain it.

It was thus with some surprise that I stood behind what was obviously a woman with a very humble background on Monday, the twenty-sixth of September 1887. Too early in the week, I hazarded, for her wages or those of her husband to have run out, and what, I asked myself, as I paid more attention to her, was she seeking to obtain an advance against?

"Mr Dyer," said she, "I found this picture while clearing out the attic. I don't know what it's worth but wondered what you could let me have against it. It looks ever so old."

"It is certainly, Mrs Blythe, not the sort of thing that you normally pledge," replied the pawnbroker. "And, if truth be told, we don't normally advance against paintings as we don't know what they are worth."

"But it's ever so pretty," she pleaded.

I looked over her shoulder to see what she was seeking to obtain an advance against.

I was a little surprised to see her judgement was sound.

The painting was a miniature, no more than a foot square surrounded by a wooden frame which had once been gilded but on which much of the gold paint was now missing. It depicted a seal which stared out of the canvas, and, rather incongruously, had a small crown perched on its head. But it was obvious that the work's creator had a mastery of portrayal as the light caught the detail both of the rather mournful-looking mammal, and of the jewels and the chasing of the crown. As I looked at the painting, I felt the beast's whiskers might start twitching, and the light illuminated the stones of the crown in such a way that I could make out each facet. What Stubbs had been to horses, the creator of this work appeared to be to this specimen of the animal kingdom.

"There's no name on it," said Mr Dyer.

"But can you give me something against it?" pressed Mrs Blythe, who was not to be put off.

"You might be better off going to an art-dealer," said Mr Dyer. "There's none round here, but you can find them in Kensington."

"What's an art-dealer? And where do you think I can find the time and the money to go all the way down to Kensington?" she snapped back.

"You want me to advance you money against a painting you have found, and I have no way of telling what it is worth."

"Well, if that's your attitude, we'll use the frame as firewood. The nights are already drawing in and it'll keep us warm for a bit in the grate."

"It's much easier advancing you money against your mangle, Mrs Blythe. But, as it's you, I can give you a pound for a week and you pay me that back plus a shilling. I suppose if you can't pay me back, I can put it in the window and see if someone wants it. A local art-fancier might like it – there are some quite well-to-do parts of town not far from here. Or an artist might be able to re-use the frame or the canvass. The risk is all mine."

What followed was what Mr Dyer trots out to every client.

"If you can't pay back the whole amount, interest will apply on the balance unpaid. So, if you pay ten shillings, you keep title to your pledge, but you'll still owe me eleven and you'll have to pay me eleven shillings and sixpence to redeem at the end of the following week."

I think a pound was more than Mrs Blythe was expecting, as she said "Done," without any haggling and was on her way.

"She always redeems," said Mr Dyer, who recognised me and was in conversational mood. "I hope she does because I don't think this painting will be easy to get shot of from here, and I don't want it cluttering up the shop. It's just as well," he added, pointing down at it, "that it's so small. At least it won't take up much space.

"But don't you like it?" I asked, for I was quite taken by the piece.

"Truth be told, Doctor," replied Mr Dyer, "I do. That was probably the real reason why I took it as a pledge. I let my feelings sway my judgement – and the longer I look at it, the more I regret my decision. Now what will it be for you? Are you popping that watch of yours again? It'll be on the usual terms."

A few minutes later and I too was out of Mr Dyer's shop, three guineas heavier and one watch lighter in the pocket.

Apart from keeping an eye on the turf and the stock market, I had at this time no means of occupying myself. Holmes and I had yet to embark on the stream of cases that were to occupy the last years of the '80s and the part of the '90s when my friend was not assumed to be dead. My financially straited circumstances, as well as my shattered health, greatly limited what I might undertake. I had found some comfort in attending services at St Marylebone Church, round the corner from Baker Street, and betook myself there on occasions, not so much because I felt any great callings of faith, but because it gave me the chance to come into contact with my fellow man without needing to spend any money. So it was now, that I attended a morning service. My fellow worshippers – I use the word in its loosest sense – for the most part also looked as though they were more interested in a cost-free way of finding company than they were in prayer and, when the plate came round for the collection, I was not the only person to offer no more than a scattering of farthings.

No one seemed interested in any sort of gathering after the service, and I returned to Baker Street to find Holmes sunk in the newspapers. He glanced at me as I entered before disappearing once more behind *The Times* but then came the remark, "So your handy guide to the turf's advice proved erroneous?"

"How the devil do you know that?" I asked, disconcerted as ever by Holmes's insights.

"Your rent is due in four days, so you need ready cash to meet it," came the voice from behind the newspaper. "When you left here earlier this morning, your watch pocket betrayed the presence of a watch. It no longer does so. Yet you are in receipt of an army pension, so you have a source of regular income, but you have obviously spent it already. And I saw you studying *The Racing Post* on Friday. A trip to the pawnbroker is the only thing that would explain your watch's absence and your need for cash can only be explained by the failure of one of the horses you have backed."

"It would be more useful, Holmes," I retorted, slightly nettled by how much Holmes knew of what I regarded as a strictly personal matter, "if you could make observations about the form of horses such as Celerity Noir before I back them rather than deduce their failure after it has happened."

The Times twitched up and down to indicate a shrug from my friend, and I dedicated myself to contemplating the racing pages of the latest set of newspapers.

But a previous bet – and, if truth be told, the reason why my pension had run out before my rent was due although I had been reluctant to give any indication to Holmes that I had another, much larger stake of which I still had hopes – bore fruit. On the twenty-eighth of September, Mandarin Lurker, whom I had backed heavily, romped away from the field in the half-past three race at Kempton Park. With my winnings, I was flush with funds and, so on the next day I returned to Mr Dyer, keen to regain my pledge.

To my surprise, I found myself again in a queue behind Mrs Blythe.

"I was pleased you liked that picture I brought in so much, Mr Dyer," said she ingratiatingly to the pawnbroker, "so I had another rummage round the attic, and look what I found!"

She reached into her bag and pulled out another painting.

This work was clearly one of a pair with the picture of the crowned seal. It was in much the same state as the previous picture she brought in – the same frame in need of the same regilding but, more strikingly, the same exquisite attention to detail in the painting. The execution rendered the mole's pelt almost tangible in its black velvetiness. And while the seal's face had borne a mournful expression, the mole, by contrast, wore a look of the breeziest exuberance on its face.

"Where do you get these paintings?" asked Dyer in some wonder.

"My husband is a servant at the Earl of Fitzroy's house at the top of Tottenham Court Road. We moved into new servants' quarters above his son's house in Covent Garden in the summer. We're right under the eaves in the piazza in Covent Garden and it's going to be cold in winter so I looked around for anything I could burn. I went through the trapdoor into the void under the tiles and found the first painting straightway. After I'd seen how much you liked it, I had another look, and found this one in a corner. There's no other painting up there though," she added, looking slightly downcast. "I had a close look."

"So these painting are not yours? You are asking me to make an advance against something you don't have good title to?"

"Well, I don't know that they belong to anyone else, since it was me who found them, and they had obviously been where I found them for a long time for they were covered with dust," said Mrs Blythe, sounding for the first time slightly unsure of herself. "If you won't lend me money against them, then I'll find someone else who will, and I'll redeem the one I gave you in the first place. You may not have many paintings in your shop, Mr Dyer, but there's no shortage of pawnbrokers in Bloomsbury, and I'm sure I'll find one to take it."

I confess I was intrigued by the paintings as I felt they might be worth more than the pawnbroker could see.

"May I look at the two paintings together?" I asked.

"Mrs Blythe, are you happy with that?" asked Mr Dyer. "I wouldn't normally show anyone else a pledged item before the term of the loan had expired."

"I'm easy," said Mrs Blythe.

I looked at the canvases and was again very taken with them. In most circumstances, I am not sure I would have done more than look, but it was rare indeed for me to have both an unencumbered claim to my watch and surplus cash in my pocket, so I said to Mrs Blythe, "I'll take both off you for two pounds."

"Done!"

And not many minutes later I was once more on the pavement with the two pictures under my arm, my watch in my pocket, and plenty of money with which to pay the rent.

I felt sufficiently buoyed by events that I went to another service at St Marylebone and, to the surprise of my fellow worshippers, left a ten-shilling note on the plate. On the way back to Baker Street I bought a copy of the Pink 'Un to see whether I could repeat my coup with Mandarin Lurker, and, in the hope of more luck, I tossed a beggar loitering at the corner of Marylebone Road and Baker Street a whole shilling. He was so surprised by my generosity, he ran up Baker Street after me, catching me at the door of 221 b, to make sure I had not made a mistake. For my part, I was so impressed by this honesty, I gave him another shilling.

When I re-entered the sitting-room at Baker Street, it was to find Mycroft rather than Sherlock Holmes in the chair beside the fireplace.

In *The Greek Interpreter*, *The Final Problem*, and *The Bruce Partington Plans*, Mycroft appears but nowhere else in the accounts of my friend's work that I have allowed to be published in my lifetime.

The occasional nature of his appearances, as my reader will have guessed, was due to the highly confidential nature of the cases in which he had a role. Mycroft was, as his brother described, the *eminence grise* of the government of whatever political colour for many generations and so the cases he brought were most secret matters of state. In fact, Mycroft often consulted with his brother from our earliest days.

"With your intellect on a significantly lower level than mine, good Sherlock," he had opined on one occasion, "and your ramifications among the lowest strata of society, you are well-placed not only to perform investigations – interview people, crawl on the floor for a fingertip search, perform research into matters of obscurity – that are not my *métier*, but also to tell me what the common man might make of my statecraft. And," he added, looking at me, "for a lack of candour in this would be absurd, it is fair to say that you, Dr Watson, may, in some respects, be even placed than my brother in the last respect."

I had put the pictures onto the table, and at Mycroft's bidding took my customary seat at the fire-place.

I had no idea where Holmes was, let alone what his brother wanted to see him about, and already knew Mycroft well enough to know not to waste time trying to make small talk.

He seemed in a state of some perplexity and drummed with his fingers against the arm-rest of the chair.

"Is he never going to come back?" he asked plaintively. "I had come to consult with him on a matter relating to the present Queen's eldest son, the Prince of Wales. I suppose," he continued, "it would not be a complete waste of time to get a general impression of him from you. What do you make of Prince Albert Edward? He will be king at some not too distant juncture."

I confess my turn in fortune had made me feel quite bullish, and I rejoindered, "I imagine he is not for nothing widely known as Dirty Bertie. But," I continued, "it is hard to see any alternative line of succession being offered."

"Indeed not, good doctor, indeed not," said Mycroft, pausing to take a pinch of snuff. "Would you care for some?" he asked, proffering the sweet-smelling tin with its dun-coloured powder, but I was already reaching for my pipe, and declined. "And it would not be credible to claim that the behaviour of Albert Edward's son, Albert Victor is any better than that of his father. I fear, we are obliged to stick close to nurse for fear of getting something worse."

Eventually he rose to leave and, as he did so, he glanced at the table. He started when he saw the pictures, but he almost immediately recovered his composure.

"Ah, Dr Watson," he purred, "I see that your investment in the turf is bringing its rewards."

"How do you know that?"

"My dear doctor," said Mycroft, "I see the *Sporting Times* or, as it is generally known form the colour of its pages, the Pink 'Un under your arm, and these pictures on your table. In my position in government, I know what an invalided-out army doctor gets. And I am sure you are far better informed than I am about the precise value of those paintings. I wish you a good day."

In *The Cardboard Box* I mentioned I had paintings on the wall of General Gordon and Henry Ward Beecher. These men had gained their fame in wartime, and I felt that the atmosphere of our sitting-room would be lightened if I replaced them with my new acquisitions. I could cheer myself by looking at the jaunty mole when I was in the red and acquire a degree of sobriety by looking at the lugubrious seal when I was in the pink. But the frames on my new acquisitions, did look rather shabby even for our distinctly lived-in living-room, and armed with some of my winnings, I went round to the art-supplies shop at the corner of York Street to get the frames regilded.

"Don't know much about painting, sir," the proprietor, Mr Greber, said, "but those two are quite striking as a pair. I can touch up those frames with gold paint for ten bob each. I'll have to get the gold paint in specially, so I'll have to ask for ten shillings in advance. So, you'll be paying half now, and half when you collect them."

I would normally have been reluctant to pay for something like this up front, but, my unwonted prosperity had, I fear, quite turned my head, and I said I would pay the whole lot straightaway.

Still feeling very buoyed by my betting coup I wondered how I might celebrate it. When I got back to Baker Street, I looked through the papers and noted that a concert at St James Hall hit exactly the right note.

1885 had been the bi-centenary of the birth of George Frederick Handel. It had revived interest not just in his oratorios, splendid as they are, but also in his instrumental pieces. 1887 saw another festival of his music and I saw that on the program for that evening were the *Water Music* and his *Music for the Royal Fireworks*. How better to celebrate my winnings than a night listening to a piece with a *Rejouissance* (meaning *Rejoicing*) as its finale?

Holmes, on his return, was pleased at what he regarded as my good fortune, though which I felt was the result of focused study of equine form, and he was as eager to hear the music as I was. When I mentioned his brother's visit, his response was, "I am sure he will be back if the matter is pressing."

With my unwonted prosperity I bought us each a concert program. The note-writer had included the following.

"Both these pieces deserve the sobriquet 'occasional'.

Before the recent revival of interest in Handel's instrumental music, this could have been taken to mean that they got no more than an occasional airing, but this happily no longer applies. These pieces are 'occasional' in the original sense of the word – they are written for special occasions.

The *Water Music* is said to have been written for a boat party from Whitehall to Chelsea hosted by George I in July 1717.

Until the arrival of railways facilitated easy transport of people and food, the Royal court was a regular traveller on the Thames as it processed from royal residence to royal residence. The court would thus move up and down the river between Windsor Castle, Hampton Court, Kingston's Bishop's Palace, Richmond (originally called Sheen and often referred to by that name), Whitehall, and Greenwich for, if it stayed in one place, it would exhaust the resources of the surrounding countryside. Thus, boat parties were a regular feature of royal life. It is therefore possible that what we have here was written for several different events although the party in 1717 is certainly the one with which this music is most associated as it is the one for which reports in early newspapers survive.

The *Fireworks Music* was commissioned in 1749 by George II for an event in Green Park to celebrate the signing of the Treaty of Aix-la-Chapelle (nowadays normally called Aachen) and the end of the War of Austrian Succession – a war that saw the last time a British monarch took to the battle field.

The selection of April for the staging of the event proved over optimistic as the evening was marred by poor weather. Most of the fireworks failed to ignite, some of the ones that did, flew off into the crowd and caused two deaths, and the stage caught fire. But this does not detract from the music commissioned with the royal instruction that only 'war-like' instruments be used – so we hear flutes, horns, hautboys in the parlance for oboes at the time, bassoons, trumpets, drums and no violins."

No such misfortunes attended the performance that we saw and, after we had supped at Goldini's, we came home in good spirits at ten o'clock.

It was when we came through the door that we realised that we had had visitors. A window at the back had been forced – the intruder had climbed onto the flat roof of a one-storey extension that stretched out into the yard at the back of 221 Baker Street.

"My winnings!" I wailed, for I had left most of my money at home.

"This looks a particularly featureless case," said Holmes said with the calm air of one whose fortune has not been purloined. "Break-ins are common and getting in from the flat roof is easy. It is fortunate that they did not want to take my violin. They probably thought they could not fence it."

"Well, you're the consulting detective. So, detect."

"The side of the window chosen to apply a chisel suggests the intruder was right-handed. He has left no smell of tobacco, so he is probably a non-smoker. He uses coal to heat where he lives as he has left some deposits when he took my Persian slipper with tobacco which, I assume he was looking to resell. Beyond that I fear I can tell you nothing. It is a burglary very neatly done. And with no distinguishing features."

If the great Sherlock Holmes was unable to help in such a crime, my reader may imagine how much less inspiring the constable was who came round. He confined his remarks to, "There's a lot of it about," and "Here's a crime number to give to your insurer." Of course, we had not thought to insure our possessions, and when I mentioned this and the loss of my winnings to the constable, he added, "Well, I doubt you would have been able to claim on your cash in any case," before heading on his way.

To have lost most of my winnings having only just won them was galling indeed, and it posed for me the awkward question of how I would pay the rent. A thought, as happy as could be obtained in the circumstances, now struck me. I could get my paintings from Mr Greber and pawn them at Dyer's, and, if he gave me a pound for each, I would, with what I still had on me, have enough to pay my rent.

I confess I was not in conversational mood when I entered Mr Greber's shop, but he almost seemed to be wating for me.

"Very interesting pictures, sir," he said. "I took the canvases out of the frames so that I could do a proper job of the gilding. I thought I'd better show you what I found written round the part of the canvas which was under the frame of the picture of the seal."

He put the canvas on the counter and written on the edge of it, previously hidden by the frame, were the following four lines.

"In the town that was once lustre,
Whence Henry climbed to see Paul,
It is there that you will find me,
Spring, winter, summer, or inglorious fall."

"I have no idea what it means," said Mr Greber.

"Have you ever seen anything like that before?" asked I, as nonplussed as he.

"I have not. Occasionally you find the name of the artist hidden away there if the picture has been badly framed there but the artist's name is the one thing that is missing even though it is a painting you'd have thought anyone would be proud of having done. What do you want me to do? Shall I put them into their frames? I've regilded them both."

I was not sure what to do. I suppose a burglary is always unexpected, but this was even more so, and then an idea struck me to improve my financial situation.

"If I take them as they are, can I have back some of what I paid you in advance."

Mr Greber looked somewhat unimpressed by this suggestion.

"I have a friend who like a puzzle," I went on. "I will show them to him. I will come back with the canvases to be framed if he says the matter is of no interest."

I was soon back at Baker Street, glad to have something to take my mind off my situation not to mention five shillings in my pocket.

I was not sure what to expect Holmes's reactions to be at my paintings – the purchase of which I was regretting as much as Mr Dyer had regretted taking them as a pledge.

In *A Study in Scarlet,* in which I first brought my friend's talents to the attention of the world, I had drawn up a list of my friend's limitations which had given him a nil or a feeble score on most areas of knowledge apart from crime and violin playing. My reader will have realised that I came to modify my view as Holmes subsequently showed knowledge on subjects as diverse as Victor Hugo, English Civil War history, and the music of the Middle Ages. In *The Hound of the Baskervilles*, the events of which occurred in 1889, although the story remained unpublished until 1901, he had seen in a series of portraits the family similarity between the original Baskerville rogue, Sir Hugo Baskerville, and the villain of the case, Jack Stapleton. But it was the knowledge of art that he displayed in that case which I would like to highlight now.

He said then, "Watson won't allow that I know anything of art but that is mere jealousy because our views upon the subject differ. Now, these are a really very fine series of portraits. I know what is good when I see it, and I see it now. That's a Kneller, I'll swear, that lady in the blue silk over yonder, and the stout gentleman with the wig ought to be a Reynolds."

I was thus hopeful that Holmes could cast a light on a matter that was all dark to me.

When I returned Holmes was behind a newspaper.

"I have a new mystery for you here, Holmes," and held up the pictures for him to see.

Holmes put down his newspapers and stared.

"Good heavens, Watson! Where did you get those?" he gasped in the end.

"I got them at the pawnbroker when I went to redeem my watch? Do you like them?"

"I am not sure that my artistic views are relevant to those paintings. Are you telling me, you fail to understand their significance?"

"What significance?"

"A crowned seal with a lugubrious expression and a mole with a happy one. Do you not see that in this conjunction, they can only tell one thing?"

"What thing? And there is a verse round the canvas. What do you make of that?"

"A verse?"

I read out:

"In the town that was once lustre,
Whence Henry climbed to see Paul,
It is there that you will find me,
Spring, winter, summer, or inglorious fall."

"Do you know any details about where they came from?"

I was baffled by Holmes's questions just as he was baffled by my failure to spot something in the paintings that was obvious to him, so this dialogue of unanswered questions continued for some time. Given how much Holmes already knows or can deduce about me, I eventually told him the details about my purchase of the paintings in the pawnbrokers, and where they had originally been found.

In return, and with the air of someone who is explaining something that should be self-evident, he said, "The mole is an animal of great significance to adherents of the Stuart or Jacobite claim to this country's throne. It was from his horse tripping over a molehill that William III, the man who ousted the last Stuart king, James II, broke his collar bone, and died from his injuries. In Jacobite circles the mole is the subject of a toast, 'To the little man in black velvet,' it runs, and the cheery expression given to the mole suggests the sympathies of the commissioner of the painting, if not necessarily of the painter, were with the Jacobite claim."

"That is surely of no more than historical interest."

"That is so. The picture of the gleeful mole does no more than set the period. It is the other picture that is of a more pressing concern. At James's fall from the throne in what has become known as the Glorious Revolution of 1688, he was reported to have thrown his royal or great seal – the seal with which he marked documents with wax to show he approved them – into the Thames with the objective of frustrating the business of government of any successor of his. The report on what happened to the Royal or Great Seal – if you write this up, you might want start capitalising the words at this point – came from adherents of King William and, without recovering the Seal from the river, was impossible to disprove."

"And what is your view on this?"

"It always struck me as unlikely that James would destroy or deliberately lose his Seal though he might wish to hide it. It was of much greater use to him and a much greater threat to his usurpers, if it remained concealed but recoverable so that it could be passed onto a successor of his choosing. I have thus always been of the view that the report that James II had thrown his Seal into the Thames was put about by adherents of the new king as a way of suggesting fecklessness in William of Orange's Stuart predecessor."

"But what relevance has this to the pictures?"

"It cannot be a coincidence that a picture showing a seal with a crown on it – in other words a royal seal, you may need to take a view on whether to capitalise that latest reference – has been found in the same location and in the same style as the picture of a mole. This picture of the seal must relate to the lost Royal Seal of James II, and this verse is a clue to where it is."

"And where is it then?"

"There's the rub. That it was the Royal Seal that is being referred to is clear from the last two lines – what the house of Orange regarded as the Glorious Revolution is what a Jacobite would regard as King James's inglorious fall. But first two lines of the verse were obviously meant as a way of saying where the Seal was hidden, and their text conveys no meaning to me. What town might once have been lustre?"

"It is beyond me."

"And me too. And even if we resolve that, we are not at the hiding place. The Royal or Great Seal is no more than a few inches across, so even identifying the town is no more than the first part of an act of discovery."

"So, where Henry climbed to see Paul means nothing to you?"

"Henry may refer to a king Henry, though the last English king of that name died one hundred and fifty years before the Glorious Revolution while the only Paul who might go without family name, is St Paul who died nearly two thousand years ago."

"What are you going to do?"

"To think. This message must have been meant to communicate with King James's descendants so I must be able to wring a meaning from it."

"I confess I was going to have the pictures reframed so that I could pawn them and so pay the rent tomorrow. Do you still need them?"

There was a pause.

"I am reluctant to have them out of here in case any further discovery I make leads me to reinspect them. I will pay your share of the rent on this occasion as long as you repay me on receipt of your next pension payment."

To be reduced to having my rent paid by my friend was a new low point for me but there seemed no alternative.

"What will you do now?" I asked.

"I will examine the atlas. I must be able to identify a town that once was lustre. I cannot believe the Seal can be hidden outside either these islands or somewhere on the western part of the continent for it was to France that James II fled after he was deposed."

So it was that Holmes got atlas after atlas and map after map off the shelves while I sat in sorry contemplation of my financial situation. He addressed not a word to me and paused only to walk up and down our sitting room or to recharge his pipe.

By the Sunday I felt in need of some sort of external comfort and again took myself off to St Marylebone Parish Church, where I sat, bored, through the first parts of the service. The Gospel reading was from the Sermon on the Mount section of Matthew, and I quote verbatim from what Matthew quotes Christ as saying on a hill located by Bible scholars as being just outside Jerusalem.

"You are the light of the world. A city set on a hill cannot be hidden. Nor do people light a lamp and put it under a basket, but on a stand, and it gives light to all in the house. In the same way, let your light shine before others, so that they may see your good."

In case I had missed the association, the vicar hammered it home in a sermon about how Christ's followers had been instructed to spread the word from Jerusalem, the shining. I confess, in my excitement, I paid scant attention to the rest of the sermon and even less to the remainder of the service, though I did note that, as if to confirm the direction of my thoughts, it ended with the hymn, *Jerusalem the Golden.* I returned to Baker Street to find Holmes still going through his maps.

"Jerusalem?" he exclaimed at my suggestion. I cannot remember a time when I have surprised him more.

"It is often called Jerusalem the shining, yet it is under Ottoman occupation so cannot be said to be shining at the moment, so it is a city that once was lustre, in the words of the verse," I interjected.

"There are many objections to your theory," said Holmes. "Jerusalem is still called Jerusalem, and to travel there to hide a Great Seal would be a hazardous undertaking even now let alone in the late seventeenth century. And who is the Henry of the second line even assuming that the Paul is St Paul."

"How often have you told me," I retorted, "that once you have excluded the impossible, whatever remains, however improbable, must be the truth? Look around you. You are surrounded by maps and atlases. Yet you have found nowhere that 'once was lustre'. I have found somewhere that can be said once to have been lustre, and which has an association with St Paul. Go to your archives and see if you can find a Henry associated with Jerusalem."

Holmes's archives were indeed a trove of esoteric information.

In *A Scandal in Bohemia* I was to find an entry relating to Irene Adler sandwiched in between that of a Hebrew rabbi and that of a staff-commander who had written a monograph upon the deep-sea fishes. Sure enough, looking for a Henry with an association with Jerusalem furnished us with a name I had never heard of – King Henry of Jerusalem – who had had that title from the end of the thirteenth century.

This discovery only served to darken Holmes's mood.

"If you are right, then this matter is at an end. I cannot journey to the Holy Land to look for this Seal even if in Jerusalem there is a place associated with this King Henry that overlooks the church of St Paul. My only hope of finding the Seal was if it were close enough to London to be accessible and in a place from where it could be abstracted."

Holmes addressed no further word to me for the rest of that day nor for all the next. He confined himself to sitting in his chair, and leafing again and again through atlases, maps, and books of reference. The closest I got to colloquy with him was when he muttered, "It cannot be Jerusalem. Why would a Jacobite go all the way there? And yet, if not there, where else?"

For my own part, Holmes's negative response to my suggestion that the town of the verse was Jerusalem made me only more downcast. How long ago seemed my betting coup and our celebratory evening of Handel's music. I still had the program and, to try and bring myself back to the happy time of the concert, I started to re-read it.

"Richmond!" I exclaimed.

"What about Richmond?"

"According to the concert program, it used to be called Sheen, and there used to be a royal palace there."

Another burrow into Holmes's archives revealed that Richmond had indeed been home to a royal residence, and that the town had borne the name of Sheen until Henry VII had changed it to Richmond to call to mind his landholdings around Richmond in Yorkshire.

"We must to Richmond tomorrow to see whence Henry climbed to see Paul."

I confess my expectations were low as we travelled down from Waterloo, but, when I somewhat sceptically asked the ticket collector at the station where Henry might climb to see Paul, he said "Ah, you mean King Henry's Mound, sir. It's up the hill to the park and turn right when you get to Richmond Gate. You should get a good view of St Paul's on a clear day like today."

And ten minutes later we were at one of London's protected views of St Paul's Cathedral – over ten miles away but its cupola picked out by the sunshine and towering over the rest of the city. It was visible through a gap in the trees – Sidmouth Wood, a bystander told us – and atop the mound the line of view was marked by a narrow flower-bed although at this early autumn season, its flowers were finished. A little plaque told us that this was one of eight protected views of St Paul's from different vantage points around London, but that this was the one furthest from the cathedral. It had got its name because it was to here that Henry VIII hastened in May 1536 to get a signal from St Paul's that his wife, Anne Boleyn had been executed, and that he was therefore free to declare his betrothal to her successor as his wife, Jane Seymour.

"This is certainly easier to get to than Jerusalem, Watson!" quipped Holmes, a note of triumph in his voice, "both for James II and for us. I will have to do some more research, but I suspect our trail is near its end. Here's five shillings. Pray get the frames restored to your paintings exactly as they were."

"With the verse covered up?"

"Exactly as they were," was all the response that I got.

Holmes was absent throughout the next day but came back just as it was getting dark, looking very pleased.

"I took the Baker Street Irregulars bulb-planting. They were directed to remove the Mound's top-soil and sift the sub-soil carefully before planting and after twenty minutes Wiggins came to me with this." He reached into his pocket and took out a hinged and rusted box. He opened it to disclose a metal disk with an embossed face on it.

"So, what are going to do with it?"

"Give me two more days."

He was as good as his word and two evenings later we sat by the fireside.

"At the turn of the seventeenth and eighteenth century in a house in the piazza of Covent Garden lived Godfrey Kneller, who was born Gottfried Kniller in Lübeck in 1646. As a German migrant, he was to portrait painting in this country in the seventeenth century what Handel was to music in he eighteenth."

"What are his best-known works?" asked I, astonished at how much Holmes had uncovered.

"As court painter, he painted portraits of both James II and of William of Orange from whom he received a knighthood. Kneller knew the value of his name and had a veritable factory of workers in his Covent Garden house painting pictures in his style. It is thus by no means certain that the pictures of the seal and the mole were by Kneller himself. Indeed, it is more likely that they were executed by one of his workers who had Jacobite sympathies or, even more probably, who had been commissioned by a Jacobite sympathiser, as I suspect not many underlings of Kneller knew or cared much about whether the House of Stuart or the House of Orange occupied the throne as long as there was a steady flow of commissions. This would also explain why such a fine pair of works should not betray who its author was."

That the paintings, still, by a matter of chance, in my possession should be valuable, was great news for me, but a pressing question occurred to me.

"How can I realise any value for these pictures? I am not even sure I have got good title to them given that they were found by someone in the service of the Earl of Fitzroy?"

At that moment there was a knock at the door.

"You asked me to come by, good Sherlock?"

"Indeed Mycroft. When you broke in here last week, you left traces of that honey-drenched snuff of yours on the sill of the window where you made your ingress. No doubt you took a pinch before forcing the frame. It would be a regrettable act to have to report one's brother to the police, but, with this evidence and, as a good citizen, I fear I might be constrained to do so."

"What do you want, Sherlock?"

"Dr Watson has related the exchange you had last week with him. In your position as the government's chief adviser, you had formed the view you had no wish for the position of the House of Saxe-Coburg to be jeopardised. When you saw pictures in Dr Watson's possession, which you read aright as threatening to resurrect interest in the House of Stuart at a time when the Prince of Wales and heir presumptive are even more mired in scandal than is normally the case, you took action to thwart it. Hence the break-in and hence the theft of my friend's money as a cover for the true reasons for your trespass."

"As I recall, Dr Watson had paintings of animals that dated from the turn of the last century. I knew they were valuable."

"And you feared that they might give an indication of where the Great Seal might be."

"I had no such indication."

"You have, dear Mycroft, always said that your intellect dwarfs mine. If I can see that a picture of a mole and a seal from the early eighteenth century are probably meant to indicate where James II's Royal Seal is hidden, then I am sure you can too although I candidly admit I have not sought to investigate the subject. Some things are best left undiscovered."

"What do you want Sherlock?"

"They are rather fine pictures, Mycroft. I am sure the government would love to get hold of them and would be willing to pay a fair price to their owner."

"I am a government advisor. How do you think I might find the money for what they are worth?"

"You audit the books of government departments. I am sure you can find not only a way for the purchase to be made but a way for it to be overlooked. The pictures could adorn the quarters of the Prince of Wales. You might like to point out to him the consequences of a member of the royal family losing the confidence of his subjects."

"And," replied Mycroft, with the air of someone eager to find the answer to a key question, but seeking to make light of it, "did you, by any chance, find any clues in the paintings as to where the Seal might be hidden."

"Dear Mycroft, I would refer you to my previous remarks. I am far too busy dealing with cases in East London to concern myself with tittle-tattle about the royal family. I leave it to you to use your grasp of statecraft to build Jerusalem in this green and pleasant land. The good Watson, whose eye for fine works of art is perhaps better than his eye for speedy horses, found the paintings and a thousand guineas would be a very reasonable price for a transfer of ownership. The location of the Seal will remain a mystery."

And so it was that my financial fortunes were not so much restored as transformed. Shortly afterwards I met Mary Morstan and, with the money for the paintings, was able to buy the medical practice I ran for the next six years until Holmes arranged for a relative of his to buy me out.

I am not aware that Mycroft ever discovered the verse telling the location of the Royal Seal. In any event, the Seal remained safely in Holmes's little museum until I put it into the tin despatch box I deposited at Cox & Co, but that night, my immediate financial future secured, I had some further questions for Holmes.

"Did Mycroft really leave traces of snuff when he broke into the flat last week."

"He did not know whether he had or had not, and presenting it as a fact gave him little choice but to confess to the break-in. And it made him far more willing to pay the price for your pictures. It may be his regard for my straightforwardness is greater than his regard for my intellect, and his estimation of both has played a crucial role on the happy resolution of this case."

"And why did you not tell him you had found the Seal?"

"Good Watson, my brother was so eager to explore the mystery of the Seal, he broke into this flat to see if the pictures would give him a clue to its whereabouts. I feel my brother is becoming a little over-mighty, and, having something I can bring out to disrupt his smooth running of the ship of state, should it be required, is most welcome."

"And might he not now dismantle the frame and find the verse?"

"He knows the pictures frames have been removed and put back on without us having given any indication that a clue to the Seal's whereabouts has been found. If he does find the verse, he will have to decrypt it. You will note that I gave him a little hint on the direction our researches had led us, although not where they finished. Even if he realises he needs to head to Richmond in England's green and pleasant lands rather than to Jerusalem in the Holy Land, he will find no Seal, and, with the plethora of bulbs planted by the Irregulars, no trace that it has been found. With that number of contingencies, I am of the view that the Seal's whereabouts are safe even from my brother."

He paused after this long speech and then concluded.

"And now Watson, if you will be kind enough to touch the bell, Mrs Hudson, who can now have some confidence on the whereabouts of her next rental payment, can bring us our supper."

A Study in Black and Orange – Afterword

The Great Seal referred to in this work remains missing.

Its original disappearance was ascribed to King James II's alleged act of throwing it into the Thames on his flight from London, but *A Study in Black and Orange* provides an alternative explanation for its whereabouts. The tin dispatch box which now holds the Seal and which Watson deposited at his bank, Cox & Co, remains untraced.

Endell Steet, where Mr Dyer's pawnbroker's shop is situated, still exists, and is mentioned in Conan Doyle's *The Blue Carbuncle*.

All the musical, historic, and artistic references, including the location of Godfrey Kneller's house and workshop in 16-17 of the Grand Piazza in Covent Garden, are accurate, and there is a plaque on the building. The first two figures in the middle row of pictures on the cover are the two kings who contested the crown in 1688 – James II and William of Orange.

The picture overleaf shows the present-day view from King Henry's Mound, where Sherlock Holmes found the Great Seal, to St Paul's Cathedral which is located over ten miles away. A trip to Richmond to see this view and enjoy the Thames-side delights of the town is well worthwhile.

The Cherry-Tree and the Comma

"Loveliest of trees, the cherry now is hung with bloom upon the bow."

It was 1916, and I had taken a constitutional walk around Bloomsbury, the parish I had come to call home after I had set up my medical practice in Queen Square following my second marriage in 1907. Easter Sunday in 1916 fell on the twenty-third of April – St George's Day – almost as late as it can be. With this late falling of the paschal feast, the cherry-blossom was at its best, and I had paused at a particularly lovely example in Russell Square as the opening of A E Housman's poem, *The Cherry*, dropped quite unbidden into my mind.

The tree's beauty, harbinger of spring at last, was, alas, out of keeping with its surroundings on that day.

Russell Square is among the grandest of central London's open spaces, but 1916 London was a city transformed compared to the metropolis of two short years before. Places of entertainment were shut, khaki-clad and alarmingly young-looking soldiers paraded down the streets from what we had been told at the war's outbreak would be but a temporary encampment on Coram's Fields, and there were sentry posts and barriers with soldiers in uniform at every corner. And on days like today, with a wind blowing in from the east, there was a constant undertone of gun-fire with the popping of artillery reports as they were carried in on the breeze across the two hundred miles which separate London from north-eastern France.

The ghostly echo of conflict in France or, I thought grimly, perhaps a portent of conflict within our own isles, rested heavily on my mind as I headed home, and I was full of foreboding when I eventually got back to Queen Square. I had barely closed the front-door when there was a peremptory knock. Standing on the step was Mycroft Holmes.

"May I come in, Dr Watson?" Mycroft (whom I will refer to by his first name to avoid confusion with his brother, Sherlock Holmes) said in an authoritative tone which suggested that a refusal would create difficulties.

"I asked brother Sherlock," Mycroft said when he was across the threshold, "to join us here. To free more men for the front, I am once more in the service of the state, but it creates less interest if I hold my more delicate meetings away from Whitehall."

Mycroft had originally been introduced to me by his brother as a minor functionary of the Civil Service, and it was only at the time of *The Bruce Partington Plans* in November 1895 that Sherlock Holmes had revealed that Mycroft was the brain whose counsel again and again decided government policy.

Once Holmes had made this revelation to me, it had become more and more obvious as the 1890s gave way to the first decade of the twentieth century that Mycroft was the hand behind every act the British government took regardless of that government's political colour. By 1916, Mycroft would have been nearly seventy. He showed his age in his bowed gait and in his high, furrowed forehead, but he retained his masterful grey eyes, and showed his customary lack of interest in making conversation as we waited for his brother.

When he arrived, Sherlock Holmes, although already sixty-two, was as spare as ever and still exuded the nervous energy of his prime.

"I see," said he to me, once he had sat down, "that your practice has benefitted from the presence in London of large numbers of soldiers wating to be sent to the front."

"It is probably as well not to say out loud why the flower of our youth would be seeking help from a doctor," chimed in Mycroft before I could say anything, "The three beads of mercury I saw between two of the floorboards at the entrance hall are very telling and make drawing an inference a facile matter."

"Gentlemen," I replied, both amused and repelled by the Holmes brothers' attempts to vie with each other on observational and deductive skills on such a subject, "I extend to my patients absolute confidentiality. I will not respond to any speculation on your part on why they should seek treatment from me."

"I would posit," said the brothers in unison, "that a deduction based on the heavy traffic of brand-new boots worn by young men who are, for the most part, new to the delights London can offer, and residual beads of mercury between your floorboards, amount to rather more than speculation."

There was a silence and then, as though impatient that presenting his petition had been delayed by the above exchange, Mycroft began.

"It is like this. The war has been going on for over a year and a half and we now have three and a half million men under arms. The men defending our island home are given little choice on what they might take with them when they go off to the front – their clothing, weaponry, and rations are standard issue – but they have a small allowance for personal items."

Mycroft paused and took a pinch of snuff before continuing.

"You, Sherlock," he said, turning to his brother, "have always had the mind for trivial puzzles. I would ask you if you might care to name the single personal item that is the most popular thing our men choose to take with them to the trenches as part of this small allowance."

"I have a mind for logical inference, good Mycroft, but not for guessing games," rejoindered his brother, I think slightly nettled. "However, your use of the term 'small allowance' suggests a soldier would want something portable, which carries happy memories of home, and which can be used to pass the lengthy times when the soldier is not engaged in combat. A pocket chess set suggests itself."

"What you say," said Mycroft, "makes sense and a pocket chess set is indeed a popular choice. But it does not meet the soldier's need for the item to be something that one can enjoy on one's own irrespective of where the winds of war might take one, be it *en route* to France, in billets, or in the trench. That requirement may explain why the most popular item is, in fact, a copy of A E Housman's collection of poetry, *A Shropshire Lad.*"

"What is the problem with that?" asked I, drawing on my pipe. "A book of poetry is easy to carry and does not require a long period of uninterrupted concentration to read. And," I added, recalling that Housman's lines had come to me only a few minutes previously, "the poetry is simple, memorable, and descriptive of the beauties of our native land."

"All those things are true," replied Mycroft, reaching into his pocket, and fishing out a slim volume with the poetry collection's name on the front. "This book has all the practical requirements you suggest and the poetry with its 'blue remembered hills' does indeed provide warm memories of our country. Moreover, there is a call to patriotic sacrifice in the poems which is unsurpassed in rival works. The third work in the set, *The Recruit* contains the lines:

> Come you home a hero,
> Or come not home at all,
> The lads you leave will mind you
> Till Ludlow tower shall fall.
>
> And you will list the bugle
> That blows in lands of morn,
> And make the foes of England
> Be sorry you were born.

Ever since its publication twenty years ago, Mr Housman has waived his royalties on this collection of sixty-three short poems, thereby not only forgoing what would be a very substantial sum of money, but also ensuring that the book is available to those of the smallest means."

"This is all very worthy," said Holmes, "but you surely have not brought me here all the way from Sussex to tell me this."

"Indeed not, dear brother" replied Mycroft loftily. "As you may imagine, mail in this country is read by the official censor. I do not intend to disclose to you what is read, but the reading is planned to maximise the chances of picking up the disclosure of information that might be of use to the enemy while minimising the resources required to capture such disclosure. Thus, for some people we read every word they write, while for others we only read their correspondence at certain times, or when they are in certain locations."

There was a pause and Mycroft pulled a slip of paper out of an inside pocket.

"In a recent letter to an associate Housman was writing about his poetry and he made the following remark. 'No doubt, I have been unconsciously influenced by Greek and Latin poetry, but the chief sources of which I am conscious are Shakespeare's songs, the Scottish Border ballads, and Heinrich Heine.' A E Housman is a great scholar of the ancient world, and is well-versed in more recent literature, but that his work is influenced by the German, Heinrich Heine, is something we find most disturbing. We cannot have a writer whose works are in the kitbags of so many of our troops tainted by a German influence. And of-course, one suspect influence raises the question of what other suspect influences or interests Mr Housman may have."

Although Holmes had been wont to quote German poetry when we had been shared quarters in Baker Street, Heinrich Heine was a name unfamiliar to me.

I think the blank look showed on my face, and Mycroft came to my rescue.

"Were we meeting in your old quarters at Baker Street, I have no doubt that my younger brother would ask you to reach into his archives and would reveal chapter and verse. And doubtless, dear Doctor, you would then entertain your readers by telling them what recondite entries were on either side of the archive entry about the poet, Heinrich Heine. The meaning of the words 'Hedonism' and 'Heist', as well as their origin, instantly suggest themselves."

He took another pinch of snuff before continuing.

"For my part, I will confine myself to telling you that Heinrich Heine was a poet of the last century. His most famous work is the *Lorelei*, a poem about a maiden who sits siren-like on a rock above the Rhine, and who lures sailors to their end with her singing. It can be read as a simple folk-tale or as an allegory on how the complaint from which Heine suffered – like the troops who are your patients – was acquired. Like Housman's poetry, the *Lorelei* has been set to music numerous times by composers both well-known and obscure. Its opening verse – I will quote it in English – is 'I know not what might be the meaning, but sadness is all that I find. A tale from ages long vanished – it will not get out of my mind' – are so well known to every German that many do not realise that it is not a folk-poem."

"I told you my brother's specialism was omniscience," said Sherlock Holmes to me from his seat, a rare smile illuminating his face.

"Thus, Housman is admitting to being influenced by a populist German poet," continued Mycroft. "This would be entirely unobjectionable at any other time, but it is of the greatest concern at this one. You cannot help but wonder what other German sympathies he may have. I do not believe we can take the risk of Housman not being..." Mycroft broke off as he sought the right word, "sound. He may produce more verse which is taken up in large numbers by our young and impressionable troops and which may have an unhelpful, unpatriotic, or otherwise seditious message behind it. We must investigate him to ensure that his work is fit to be in the kitbag of our troops."

"What do you want us to do?" asked Sherlock Holmes, and I felt my heart quicken at the prospect of working with my friend again.

"Housman lives in Cambridge," Mycroft replied, "where he is a Professor of Classics at Trinity College. He will be engaged in giving classes all morning on Monday week – that is to say, the first of May. While he is teaching, I want you to search his quarters to find out anything you can about him – it is as well to keep such sensitive activities in the hands of agents whom one can trust. I have spoken to the Dean of Trinity College. Your entry to Housman's quarters will be facilitated by the College and there will therefore be no need to for you to do any breaking and entering."

My readers will understand that the precise detail of our ingress to Housman's rooms must remain a secret, but I would draw their attention to a most significant matter that arose on Easter Monday, the twenty-fourth of April. The so-called Easter Uprising broke out in Dublin, and London newspapers were full of reports of death among the population and the destruction of the centre of the city. The rebellion was put down by the end of the month with many of the ring-leaders facing the firing squad after a court martial.

I was perturbed that my Easter Sunday premonition of warfare in our isles should have been realised so rapidly and in such an unexpected way and, right up to the time to catch our train from King's Cross to Cambridge, I wondered whether the Uprising might cause a postponement or cancellation of our planned break-in. But, just as Mycroft had ordained, ten o'clock in the morning of the first of May 1916 saw Holmes and me heading up the stairs from the central court at Trinity College, and into Housman's rooms. The poet's quarters consisted of a sparsely furnished bedroom, and a large study filled from floor to ceiling with books.

"I will go through Housman's desk and correspondence," said Holmes with his customary incisiveness. "You see if you can find anything of concern on his bookshelves, good Watson."

I was not really sure what I should be looking for.

The first book I came across was a slim black volume marked Accounts Book which I slipped into my pocket before I realised the impracticality of taking such an approach when weighty tomes lined two walls of the room. I decided, in the end, to note down the authors who were of interest to Housman – I had noted volumes by Aeschylus, Apollinaire, Ariosto, Aristophanes, Baudelaire, Burns, Coleridge-Taylor, Dante, and Donne among other books which on inspection proved to be works on the textual analysis of ancient manuscripts. I was progressing to Eichendorff and Euripides when we heard a key in the lock and the door to the study flew open. Dressed in an academic gown and mortar board, the moustached figure in his mid-fifties framed by jambs and lintel could only be Housman.

"Mr Holmes and Dr Watson," said he in a tone that betrayed recognition of us rather than surprise at our intrusion. "I know your faces from the illustrations in the Strand magazine to which I have long subscribed, and I have always harboured the desire to meet you," he continued as if in explanation. "I confess I had always thought that some of my activities might be subject to investigation, and I am rather flattered that this investigation has been entrusted to two investigators as illustrious as yourselves to conduct."

The professor lit his pipe before he began speaking again.

"It is thus a matter to be rejoiced that I cut short my lectures. The call for men to serve in the forces meant that there were only women among the students this morning. I very much fear that if I am forced to remember which student is Miss Jones and which is Miss Robinson, I shall probably start to confuse the second and fourth declensions. I therefore brought my teaching to a swift conclusion and find that I am far better rewarded by meeting two individuals in whose activities I have always taken the keenest interest."

"What makes you think you might be investigated?" I heard myself asking, somewhat bewildered by the professor's equanimity at our intrusion.

"When I was one-and-twenty," replied our interlocutor, "I heard a wise man say, 'Give crowns and pounds and guineas, but not your heart away, Give pearls away and rubies, But keep your fancy free...'"

His voice trailed away, and Housman paused to draw on his pipe. It was a full minute before he finished his poem, and his voice faded in a forlorn diminuendo as he completed the last line.

"But I was one-and-twenty, no use to talk to me."

He paused again.

"At twenty-one," he continued, "a love came over me such as perhaps only comes to anyone once in a lifetime. My love was not reciprocated, but while the object of my desire lives, I will not embark on another attachment as I know that none can equal the power of what I felt then and continue to feel now. As my love is probably the reason for your presence here in my study, it will not be a surprise to you if I say that the object of my desires was a man by the name of Moses Jackson, a scholar and athlete, who is now married and lives in Canada."

Holmes remained silent, and I think he was wise to do so as Housman continued in a sombre tone and with a downcast gaze.

"That was over a quarter of a century ago. Since then, I have drawn comfort from reading, editing, and translating the verse of the ancient Greeks and the ancient Romans. Some of the ideas in that verse have informed my own poetry output much of which is too personal to publish but which I, in any case, regard as secondary to the editions of the works of the ancient writers – Juvenal, Propertius, and Manlius – that are my main output. But sometimes I come up with a work which gives vent to my feelings without the true import of those feelings being too obvious in the text. And then I publish it." He puffed again on his pipe. "I have, it is true, claimed influences from sources other than the Latin and Greek poets, but that was largely as a means of deflecting too much interest into my works' true meaning."

Holmes glanced briefly at me before saying, "I am not sure, Professor, that there is much purpose to be served in prolo…"

But Housman was not to be stopped. It was almost as if he were glad to get the matter off his chest.

"You gentlemen may as well know the full details of why the authorities are interested in me. My love is not acceptable to British tastes, and I actively suppress my inclination when in this country. But, before the current conflagration, I used to go to France every summer where, amongst other things, I would go for walks, pursue my interests in gastronomy, and read books that are of too controversial a nature to be published here. And at every turn I looked for faces that reminded me of the object of my desires. It is probably for these diversions that the authorities are taking an interest in me now."

Holmes rose to go, and I followed his example, but Housman carried on, his eyes three-quarters closed as if in reverie.

As we stood at the threshold, I heard him say as though to himself, "Because I liked him better, than it suits a man to say, it irked him, and I promised to throw the thought away. To put the world between us we parted stiff and dry, 'Farewell,' said he, 'forget me.' 'Fare well, I will,' said I."

Holmes put his fingers to his lips as he quietly closed the door and, even as we stood in the corridor, we could hear Professor Housman continue to quote from his own verse. "If here, where clover whitens..." were the last words I heard as we headed back down the stairs.

Holmes telegraphed from Cambridge Station and Mycroft came to meet us at Queen Square.

"Well, if Housman's amatory preferences is all we have to worry about, we can consider the matter closed," my friend's elder brother said dismissively. "There are, it is true, lots of references to love between men in *A Shropshire Lad*, but they can all be seen in the spirit of soldierly or rustic comradeship which is not unhealthy during the current emergency when our men are under arms and most come from farmsteads across the land. Spartan military success was positively fuelled by such soldierly bonds. And there are enough somewhat cliched references to love between lads and lasses and dreams of rose-lipt maidens" – Mycroft uttered these last comments in a way that made clear his indifference to such softer feelings – "for our men to think nothing but wholesome thoughts of home when they are in Flanders."

It was only when I was walking the Holmes brothers to the front-door that I remembered the Accounts book which I had abstracted.

"I haven't looked at this," I said, taking it out of my inside pocket, "but I did think that if Housman had been receiving payments from a foreign power, it might disclose them. In the circumstances perhaps it would be best if this be returned to Housman."

I handed the book to Mycroft who opened it. "It seems to be a journal of payments. They are all made in France."

He looked again and then read out.

"'July 23rd, 1906 La Baule, the fisher-boy 10 shillings.' 'August 16th, 1907 Le Touquet – the sommelier – 12 shillings.' 'September 9th, 1908 Cannes – the pastry chef – 11 shillings'." My friend read out further entries, the contents of which I would not wish to disclose.

There was a silence as the import of the black book sank in.

"Well," said Mycroft drily, "Professor Housman certainly seems to have a catholic taste in the delights a French seaside resort can offer. I note," he continued, flicking through the book, "that all the entries here are referenced to France so no offence is recorded in this country. That seems to confirm what Housman told you about how and where he..." Mycroft broke off to consider what the *mot juste* might be, "indulges his predilections. I think that merely underlines the wisdom of my previous statement that the matter is closed."

He paused to consider his next comment.

"I think however, it would be as well in the current climate if I retained this book," he said at last, and he slipped it into an inside pocket. "I am sure it will be the first thing that Housman will have looked for after you had gone. Its absence will tell him not only that whatever other influences he may seek, they must not be of a type which attracts the attention of the authorities, but also that not much escapes the attention of those authorities. That further strengthens my conviction that it is safe to allow *A Shropshire Lad* to remain in circulation – indeed its withdrawal when it is so well-known would raise questions even more difficult than its continued distribution."

I thought our encounter with Mycroft at Whitehall had brought the matter on which we had been commissioned to an end, but what happened next is an illustration of Mycroft's power and guile which may simultaneously comfort and disconcert my reader.

In the foregoing I have referred to the Uprising in Dublin which was put down with a force and swiftness that was exemplary in every sense of the word. Even before the Easter Monday launch of the Uprising, the British government had known that something was afoot in Ireland as on the Good Friday, so, the twenty-first of April, a British diplomat of Irish origin, Sir Roger Casement, had been arrested after he had put ashore from a German U-Boat on the Kerry coast.

Casement had had a brilliant career in the British diplomatic service. He had done much good humanitarian work identifying abuse of native labourers and their families in possessions of European empires in the Congo and in Peru. For this work, he had been knighted in 1911.

But by this time, he had already embraced the cause of Irish nationalism, and in 1913 he helped found the paramilitary force, the Irish Volunteers. The outbreak of hostilities in August 1914 saw him meeting German diplomats in New York to fix a deal whereby Germany would provide arms to the Irish who would in turn revolt against British rule. Casement then travelled to Germany via neutral Norway and tried to raise an Irish army amongst Irish troops held in German prisoner of war camps.

Thus, while many of the Easter insurrectionists were subject to summary trial and execution by firing squad, Casement had already spent three days in custody at the Uprising's outbreak. He was detained first in the Tower of London and then, for fear that his state of mind might lead him to take his own life, at Brixton Prison. His trial on a charge of high treason at the Old Baily was held in June 1916.

This formal trial caused considerable legal difficulty for the prosecution.

The only legislation that could be found which appeared to cover the offence of seeking to raise an army against the King was a law from the time of Edward III which was a translation of a text originally in Norman French. The French and English text were unpunctuated, but the following text was put before the court. It defined a treasonable act as being committed:

"if a Man do levy War against our Lord the King in his Realm, or be adherent to the King's Enemies in his Realm, giving to them Aid and Comfort in the Realm or elsewhere."

Casement's counsel, Mr Sergeant Sullivan, argued that the legislation created two offences. That of levying war against the King in his realm, and that of adhering to the King's enemies in his realm. He further posited to the court that the words, "giving to them Aid and Comfort in the Realm or elsewhere," were by way of explanation of how assistance (adherence) might be given to the King's enemies. He proposed to the court that the assistance had to have been given within the King's realm for the offence of treason to have been committed, and accordingly submitted that the indictment for treason should be thrown out as Casement's acts had been committed outside the King's realm.

The counsel for the prosecution persuaded the court to read a comma between the third iteration of the word "Realm" and "or" so that the text could be read to apply to acts committed outside the King's realm.

The jury seemed to see no difficulty in applying the prosecution's interpretation of a law written over half a millennium previously to deal with a recently committed act. A guilty verdict was passed after deliberations lasting less than an hour and a capital sentence imposed which was confirmed at an appeal before five House of Lords judges. Casement was moved to Pentonville Prison and given the customary three Sundays from the confirmation of his sentence to make his peace. His execution was scheduled for the third of August.

I thought the matter closed and I confess I thought the arguments of Casement's counsel to have been the merest casuistry. Logical extension of Sullivan's argument would mean that a charge of treason could not be brought against a woman, and the law had clearly been framed to capture a wide range of acts.

It was on the evening of the thirty-first of July, as I was having my last pipe of the day, that there was a knock on the door. On the step stood Mycroft who again asked to be admitted with an authority that could not be denied.

"The verdict," he began without preamble, "in Casement's trial has caused considerable resentment in Ireland, and unease in countries around the globe. We are going to have to clear up the mess."

I was unable to understand why that should be the case.

"The leaders of the Uprising have been summarily dealt with," I expostulated. "I have no doubt that among those men who faced the firing squad, there were some more deserving of their fate than others. Casement, by contrast, has received a full trial, and the verdict and sentence have been the subject of an appeal. There was no dispute on the facts, and the legal technicality advanced by his counsel as to why he should be acquitted seems to me to have been made because there was no other defence available. I am sure that any British tommy who tried to raise an army among British prisoners of war would face a court-martial on the day of his capture, and a firing squad at dawn the day after, no matter where he tried raise such an army. There will be outrage across the land if Casement is not dealt with as the court has directed."

"Quite so, dear Doctor, quite so," soothed Mycroft. "Anger in mainland Britain is to be avoided at all costs while resentment in Ireland is something that we can live with. What is of far greater concern is the effect of our behaviour on perceptions of this country in the United States. Our main foreign policy objective is to secure American involvement on our side in this war. Anything that smacks of the martyrdom of Casement is to be avoided as it will attract huge opprobrium among Irish-Americans whom it is important not to alienate in advance of the presidential elections this November."

"So, are you expecting to meet your brother here? Is he going to resolve matters? And is there any help required from me?" I asked, wondering where this was heading, and used to – though perhaps not reconciled to – the Holmes brothers using my property as a convenient meeting point whenever they chose.

"No, Dr Watson, it is your help I would like in this matter. I can see no role for my brother. We wish both so to destroy Casement's reputation as to undermine the cause of Irish independence, and yet for him to escape what would be the normal consequences of his action to avoid a negative reaction in the United States."

Sherlock Holmes had always been slighting about my abilities as an investigator. I was therefore at a loss how I could help his even more gifted brother achieve what appeared to me to be two contradictory objectives.

I think Mycroft saw my hesitation for he quickly expanded on what he was looking for.

"Casement is in the condemned man's cell at Pentonville. I am going to meet him there tomorrow and make him a proposition that he might or might not take up. If I were to go with a British civil servant as a witness, the general public may not believe what will subsequently be reported. But if it is Dr Watson – a man whose reputation for truth and decency is unassailable – who delivers the report on our meeting, then no one will be inclined to disbelieve it."

"And what if I should decline to help you? I cannot see why I should be involved in an attempt to thwart the workings of justice to enable us to ingratiate ourselves with the Americans."

"My dear Dr Watson, you have described me as *being* the British government. With an eminence such as that, you can imagine how, if you do as I say, I can make your life very pleasant even at these hardest of times, and how, if you decline, I can make your life very hard even at the pleasantest of times."

So it was that the next morning saw me meet Mycroft at the forbidding gate of Pentonville prison, and, after the completion of security checks, we were soon in front of the bearded Casement as he sat with two guards in the cell next to the gallows. He had obviously not been advised that he was about to receive a visit from a representative of the British government, let alone that I would be in attendance, and he looked at us in some bewilderment.

"Mr Casement," (Casement had been stripped of his knighthood when he had been condemned to death) began Mycroft, once the guards had left the three of us on our own, "whatever your offences, it is not in the British government's strategic interest for you to be executed. I am here to make you an offer which, if you accept, will enable us to commute your sentence. Dr Watson is here as a witness who can be relied upon, and who will publish a record of our discussions, assuming we can come to an accommodation."

"I am listening, Mr Holmes," said Casement in a soft voice with a distinct southern Irish lilt.

"At your trial and subsequent appeal your defence council was remiss in not drawing the court's attention to your state of mind. A plea of 'guilty but insane' might have been accepted by the court. Even now, if a plea of insanity were put forward by the defence as a reason for your actions, the prosecution would accept it, and the revised verdict would not even have to go in front of a jury which may be less willing to take a strategic view of your actions than the British government does. Your record as a diplomat, statesman, and humanitarian is of such merit that your most recent deeds can readily be attributed to a health-induced eclipse of your mental faculties."

"The only maladies I suffered in the whole episode of my journey from Germany to Ireland on the submarine and in my time on land before capture, were sea-sickness from the tossing of the U-Boat, and then malaria fever on land which I have suffered from ever since my time in the Congo. While I was in Germany before embarking the submarine, I enjoyed excellent health. I was entirely clear in what I was doing. I would not wish to undermine the cause of Irish independence by saying I acted as I did while temporarily insane."

Casement held us in a steady gaze and Mycroft tried another gambit.

"Mr Casement, after your capture, your London flat was subjected to a thorough search. Amongst your papers was found a diary recording the lowest forms of sexual encounters with other men."

"It's a lie!" retorted Casement.

"I can read you extracts," said Mycroft smoothly, and fished what I recognised instantly to be Housman's dairy out of his pocket. He read the extracts that he had previously read when I had first handed him the book though I noted he omitted the times and places of the encounters described.

"When did you forge this document?" asked Casement fiercely.

"My dear Mr Casement, this diary was found on the first of May. Are you really telling me that the British secret service is capable of forging such a work in the ten days between your arrest and this book's discovery?"

"I have nothing to say."

"Very well, Mr Casement. I do have something to say, and I will say it. If you admit to the authorship of these diaries, your punishment for seeking to raise an army in Germany among Irish prisoners of war to fight against British forces will be commuted to one of confinement to a secure establishment for an undefined period on the grounds of insanity. By the time this country is triumphant in its war against the Central Powers, I confess it may no longer be in my gift to release you, but I shall be very surprised if that is not precisely what is done."

"But those faked diaries will result in the trashing of my reputation and, by association, the trashing of the cause of an independent Ireland."

"I am very confident of the true provenance of these diaries, Mr Casement. They were found by two of the Government's most trusted agents on the date stated. And I am very sure that your authorship of such diaries will be readily accepted by the public. It will be noted that that you are an unmarried man, and many will observe that your long record of work among the down-trodden provides you with many opportunities to extract, shall we say, personal favours in exchange for the provision of help. Some may conclude you undertook the work you did precisely to gain opportunities to extract such favours."

There was a long silence and then it was Casement who asked a question of Mycroft.

"Mr Holmes, why is Great Britain fighting this war?"

"I can do no better than to quote the words of our prime minister, Mr Asquith. He said, 'We are fighting to vindicate the principle that small nationalities are not to be crushed, in defiance of international good faith, by the arbitrary will of a strong and overmastering power.'"

"That principle does not seem to extend to Ireland," retorted Casement. "The Germans, by contrast, have stated that they desire only Irish national prosperity and national freedom."

"I have no doubt that the Belgians and the Luxembourgers, the violation of whose neutrality was the *casus belli* of this war, would regard the German expression of such a desire with a due degree of scepticism."

There was another long silence.

"Mr Holmes," said Casement, "if I accept your offer, the cause, for which I was fully aware I was risking my life, will be set back by a hundred years. You have had to rewrite the law of the land in order to find me guilty of any offence, and you now want me to admit to other trumped-up offences to avoid a political embarrassment."

"You have never sought to deny that you tried to raise an Irish army in Germany to fight in Ireland against the British army. That can only help the Germans as it would use British manpower that could otherwise be used to fight against them. It was an act of betrayal to this country far worse than these amorous adventures on which it would have been far easier to prosecute you."

"The court that tried me, an Irishman, was not a jury of my peers. I have a right, an indefeasible right, if tried at all, to be tried in Ireland, before an Irish court and by an Irish jury. The court that tried me cannot but be prejudiced in varying degree against me, most of all in time of war. I would accept the verdict of a jury of my own countrymen, be it Protestant or Catholic, Unionist or Nationalist, Sinn Fein or Orangemen."

"But Ireland has been promised home rule," said Mycroft, a sudden note of pleading in his voice. "When that comes, most legislation for Ireland will be enacted by an Irish government elected by the Irish themselves. Sinn Fein means 'we ourselves', and it will be the Irish who will be governing themselves."

"We have been told," replied Casement, "we have been asked to hope, that after this war Ireland will get Home Rule, as a reward for the lifeblood shed in a cause which whomever else its success may benefit can surely not benefit us. It is not necessary to climb the painful stairs of Irish history to review the long list of British promises made only to be broken, of Irish hopes raised only to be dashed to the ground."

"You seem, if I may so, Mr Casement," replied Mycroft, "to be totally divorced from the realities of Irish public opinion. There was no mass uprising after the Dublin insurrection of Easter Monday. The uprising was largely confined to the centre of Dublin and was put down within a week, while brave and loyal Irishmen continue to go in their thousands to the front line against the Central Powers."

"If Irishmen go by the thousand to die, not for Ireland, but for Flanders, for Belgium, for a patch of sand on the deserts of Mesopotamia, or a rocky trench on the heights of Gallipoli, they are said to be winning self-government for Ireland. But if they dare to lay down their lives on their native soil, then they are traitors to their country, and their dream and their deaths alike are phases of a dishonourable fantasy. If it be treason to fight against such an unnatural fate as this, then I am proud to be a rebel, Mr Holmes, and I shall cling to my 'rebellion' with the last drop of my blood."

"And that is your last word? You will not admit to the authorship of these diaries and so save your life?"

"I will not admit to it. I will not tell a lie to save my neck."

"We could if you wish," and I could tell from his tone that Mycroft was making his final offer, "say that it is believed the content of this diary merely represented your aspirations and not your actions. And that these fantasies, for fantasies they are, reflect your disturbed state of mind. That way most people would not believe that this diary was a record of actual deeds and would make your plea of insanity more plausible. I am sure Dr Watson here could be prevailed upon to write a report on this meeting to carry precisely this construction. And his word has a credibility that no one would disbelieve it."

Casement rose to his feet.

"Sir, I would rather be hanged on a comma, for that is what will happen to me now, than admit to the authorship of these diaries that are not from my hand, and which will discredit both me and my cause. I would wish you two gentlemen a good day. I have a long journey before me, and I must ensure that my preparations for it are complete."

I was not sure what to say as Mycroft and I left the prison, but Mycroft seemed uninhibited by self-doubt.

"My brother has always said that the press is useful when you know how to use it. I will make sure that the contents of this Accounts book – I think I shall call it the Black Diary – are with the editor of every national newspaper within the day. I do not think the calls for clemency being made by people intelligent enough to know better – WB Yates, George Bernard Shaw, the United States Senate, and the rest – will be sustained once these diaries are public knowledge. Thus, irrespective of Casement's stubbornness in his reaction to my offer, the matter can be turned to the benefit of the British government. Just as if Casement had been persuaded to take the coward's way out, that would also have been turned to the British Government's advantage."

He paused to take a pinch of snuff before continuing.

"And I would reiterate to you Dr Watson the consequences of a word out of place from you about the matter to which you have just been a witness."

He turned and strode off with a vigour which belied his years while for my own part I was bewildered by the turn of events.

I confess that my opinion of the justice of the sentence passed on Casement was unshaken. This it was that had prevented me raising the inconsistency of Mycroft taking no action against Housman on acts committed overseas, but letting Casement go to the gallows when the latter's offences had taken place "outside the realm". And for all that I regarded Casement's action as treasonous, it was impossible not to admire the condemned man's commitment to his beliefs, and his courage in the face of an opportunity to escape the gallows at the cost of his reputation.

Yet while it sticks in my craw to say so, Mycroft Holmes's opportunism quite took my breath away. It was impossible to applaud his tactics, but it was equally impossible not to admire his Machiavellian skill in statecraft. I had no way of telling even whether Mycroft's commission to Holmes and me on Easter Sunday 1916 had anything to do with Housman in the first place or whether it had really been a quest to find a document with which to traduce Casement who had already been under arrest for two days at the time of Mycroft's first visit to Queen Square.

It has been several months before I have taken the courage to make a record of events as I take Mycroft's word about the all-seeing eye of his agents seriously. I am penning these last words at a quarter to three on Maundy Thursday, the fifth of April 1917. I shall then walk the short distance down to Charing Cross and have this work added to those in my despatch box at Cox & Co just before it closes for Easter. For all his cunning, I do not believe that Mycroft will be able to retrieve it from there.

These last paragraphs I am setting down under the same cherry tree I stood under at the start of this narrative and, like the narrative voice of Heinrich Heine's poem, my confusion of feelings means I am not sure why I feel so sad. Is it the inevitable death of a brave man, the use of the lowest and yet most effective form of political guile by Mycroft, or the pervasive gloom of this seemingly unending war?

The cherry's buds are still tight closed – Easter is over two weeks earlier than last year and it has been a cold start to spring. The words of the first verse of Housman's poem about the cherry-tree are perhaps worth quoting in full as I contemplate how a man who believed in his cause went to his end.

> Loveliest of trees, the cherry now
> Is hung with bloom along the bough,
> And stands about the woodland ride
> Wearing white for Eastertide.

The Cherry-Tree and the Comma - Afterword

Casement and Housman are the two figures in the bottom row of portraits on the front cover. Dr Watson's account covers personalities and events that are reasonably well-known but the link between Casement's black diaries and Housman's Account Book, in which the latter detailed his amorous adventures, is revealed here for the first time.

Readers may be interested in the painting below by John Lavery showing Casement's appeal to the House of Lords. Casement is at the back of the picture.

M Harris Smith

My friend's financial situation has long been a subject of speculation among his many followers.

Early in his career, he described himself as the world's only consulting detective and commented that whenever either Lestrade or Gregson was at a loss in a case – their normal state, Holmes drily opined – they would come to Baker Street to consult him, and that was how he earned his bread and cheese.

My more observant readers will have realised the implausibility of this statement as a way of explaining how Holmes made a living. Lestrade and Gregson would not themselves have been in a financial position to reward Holmes for any consultancy services he provided. Nor would Scotland Yard have looked favourably on an expense claim containing charges tendered by my friend for his services. And yet in no case save in *The Priory School*, where Holmes pocketed £12,000, did he claim a significant reward for his services. It is perhaps no coincidence that this case occurred in 1903, right at the end of the time span from which I chose to draw accounts of my friend's adventures, for, rendered financially secure by this reward, Holmes largely withdrew from criminal detective work after this time.

Yet, in spite of my friend's apparently minimal income, his outgoings were considerable.

He paid for the rooms in Baker Street, sometimes on his own at the times I was married, and he conducted cases, often travelling overseas to do so. He did all this while also paying rent on no fewer than five hidey-holes round London which he could visit to change his disguise.

This disjunction between his income and his outgoings has led to suggestions that he may have used his extraordinary skills to enrich himself in ways that I forbore to disclose in my accounts of his activities. I would point out that at the time of *The Final Problem*, my colleague stated that he had always used his powers on the right side. The case that follows not only confirms this to be so, but also explains one of the sources of income which gave my friend the financial independence that enabled him to provide his detective services, as he described them, upon a fixed scale unvaried save when he chose to remit them altogether.

No one could levy the charge against my friend that he was in any way lacking in financial acumen. On the contrary his cases often required him to display a deep understanding of finance – whether to trace cheques made out to a bogus third party with the purpose of depleting an estate in *The Norwood Builder*, or to carry out research into the financial background of Dr Roylott in *The Speckled Band*. Perhaps his greatest display of financial guile, is his often-overlooked betting coup in the race that followed Silver Blaze's win in the Winchester Cup. On this later race, my friend so timed the placing and the amount of his stakes on different horses that, at the drop of the flag, he stood to make money no matter which one won the race.

My wife Mary went away to take the waters in the early summer of 1889. It was felt better to close up the house in her absence from domestic duties although my medical practice in Paddington remained open. Accordingly, I moved temporarily back to Baker Street and returned to my practice only to minister to my patients. These were at that time few in number, and in the end I spent most of my time at Baker Street as I had as a bachelor.

Then it was that the *Silver Blaze* case arose.

It was on the morning of Friday the twenty-eighth of June 1889, the day after the conclusion of that case, that I opened the newspaper to see the following announcement:

> We are happy to announce the impending flotation on the London Stock Exchange of **Marylebone Coal Supplies Limited**.
>
> With the recent expansion of the Great Central Railway Company's activities out of Marylebone Station to take in routes through the Chilterns to Birmingham and beyond, we, as the chief suppliers of coal for the trains running out of the station, see great prospects for our business, for which it will require outside capital beyond the means of the company's current shareholders.
>
> We have, accordingly, decided to offer shares in our company to the general public.

There followed a series of tables showing impressive growth prospects for Marylebone Coal Supplies over the coming years, although the results for previous years showed only modest advancement. The announcement dwelt on opportunities offered by the expansion of Marylebone Station and advised it was in the process of adding ancillary businesses to its portfolio.

The growth prospects had been endorsed by the company's new auditors, Harper Sanderson & Co, who were taking over from the previous audit firm, M Harris Smith. The company explained the change by its desire to have its activities regulated by a firm that was a member of the Institute of Chartered Accountants and thanked the retiring audit firm for its previously rendered services.

As my reader will be aware from my flirtation with the purchase of South African stocks, and by a later poor investment making it impossible for me to take a holiday, I have always had an eye for speculative stocks and shares. Accordingly, the prospect of investing in a business supplying coal to what was described as London's fastest growing rail terminus, immediately caught my attention. I perused the financial details the company had published and looked at its impressive plans for growth and its dividend prospects.

For his part, Holmes, having taken in the agony columns and scanned the papers in vain for anything of a criminal nature, had lapsed into the state of lassitude that was often his way after the conclusion of a difficult case. I kept a weather eye on him as I knew that such a mood was dangerous to one for whom the needle remained an attractive way dealing with a sudden relaxation of tension that the end of a case brought. I knew that repose, eschewing exhilaration caused either by cocaine or by a new investigation, was the best way of maintaining my friend's equilibrium.

It was thus with a look of quite unearned reproach that I greeted our latest client when there was a knock on our door.

Before I could say anything, however, Holmes bade our petitioner cross the threshold, and he sat down.

"My name is Grant Whistler," said he, "and I have a most peculiar matter to relate. I wanted to seek your advice, Mr Holmes, as a man of the world."

As is my custom, I eyed our client to see what I could deduce from him, but I saw nothing beyond a solid bewhiskered member of the bourgeoisie. Holmes noted my activity and smiled.

"I can see that you are perturbed, Mr Whistler," replied my friend, "It is a pleasure to be petitioned by a near neighbour. And it is with concern that I note that the reason for your disquiet is something that arose on your street in the night just past, as anything that has an adverse effect on where you live is likely to affect us here in Baker Street as well."

Our petitioner started at Holmes's aperçu, and Holmes smiled as he leant back in his chair.

"I see adhering to your shoe, Mr Whistler, a tallow stain from a candle but you are otherwise neatly dressed. I cannot believe that a tallow stain would have been allowed to remain long on your shoe. And it would only have got there if you had been carrying a candle while out on your street. And it would not still be adhering to your shoe, if you had come any distance to consult with us, or if you had permitted any significant effluxion of time between what caused your disturbance, and your referral of the matter to me. Hence my deductions that your disturbance dates from the night just past, from the immediate vicinity of where you live, and that you are a near neighbour of ours here in Baker Street."

"What you say is all true," said our petitioner. "I live on Houston Close and so within a few hundred yards of your door. Houston Close is one of the roads running into Marylebone High Street. As its name suggests, it is closed to through traffic and would be the quietest of streets were it not for the presence at its end of the premises of Marylebone Coal Supplies Limited. This is a growing business and supplies coal for the trains at Marylebone Station as well as providing coal to local houses."

Mr Whistler paused in the presentation of his disquisition and Holmes took the opportunity to light his pipe.

"Houston Close is a residential street and I have the honour," Mr Whistler raised his hand to his mouth to give a discrete cough as he said this, "to be the Chairman of its Residents' Association. As the only business in a residential street, the activities of Marylebone Coal Supplies Limited are tightly controlled. It is not allowed to transport coal during the hours of darkness, and it needs the agreement of the Association if it wishes to diversify – as I think the specialist commercial term is – the scope of its business activities."

Mr Whistler paused again.

"I live at number 16 which is the last one on the south side of the street before the premises of Marylebone Coal Supplies Limited. I sleep at the front of the house, and I have a restless sleep. Last night I woke to the sound of horses' hooves in the street. As the Chairman of the Residents' Association, I felt it was incumbent on me to find out what was going on. I pulled on a dressing gown and my shoes, lit a candle, and went down onto the street. When on the street, I held my candle aloft."

I listened agog to learn what Mr Whistler might have seen.

"In the candle's feeble light," our petitioner continued, "I saw proceeding down the road, a large horse-omnibus of the type you see every day on the streets of London conveying people to their destinations when the Underground does not provide the most convenient means of transport. The gates of the Marylebone Coal Supplies Limited's premises stood open, and the omnibus went through it. As I stood there, another drove past me and into the yard, and then a third. The gates of the yard then clanged shut. As I had been woken up before I went down, I can only conclude that there are at least four horse-buses in the company's yard."

Mr Whistler took a pinch of snuff before continuing.

"I waited to see if any more traffic would come down the street, but none did. I was about to go back indoors when I noted a faint smell of hot metal carried on the breeze. I paused, and as I did so, I saw a dark-lantern, the source of the hot metal smell, shine out. In the light it threw, I saw the lantern was in the hand of a woman who was standing by the gates on the other side of the road. She was turned away from me and facing the gates. She gave no sign of seeing me, but, as I watched, she put the lantern on the ground, crouched by it, and I observed her making an entry into a notebook. I was sufficiently shaken by events that I withdrew into my house, and this morning, after my disturbed sleep, I have come to you."

"And what is your concern, Mr Whistler?" asked my friend.

"It is not my desire to interfere with the workings of the Marylebone Coal Supplies or of Marylebone Station without good cause," said our petitioner. "Each is a major employer in Marylebone, and indeed some of the senior staff of both organizations live on Houston Close. At the same time, the value of the properties in our road depends on Marylebone Coal Supplies working in a way that recognises its privileged position of being a business – and an intrusive one at that – in a residential area. I would like you to review its activities and make a recommendation to me on how I should proceed as Chairman of the Resident's Association – whether to ignore what has happened until there is more than one night's disturbance of our slumbers, or to make immediate representations to the management."

"You make yourself very plain. And have you yourself formed your own view of what might be going on?"

"Well, I really came here to obtain your opinion, Mr Holmes, rather than to propose one myself. But with the growth of traffic from Marylebone Station, a horse-omnibus service facilitating easy transfer for travellers between Marylebone, Paddington, Euston, St Pancras, and King's Cross Stations, is an obvious suggestion for all that running such a service out of Houston Close would be a clear breach of the Marylebone Coal Supplies' covenants and articles of association. Indeed, I can see no other purpose to the delivery of horse-omnibuses to these premises, and to run its existing business, the company already has stables, grooms, coachmen, and a smithy, and so would be well placed to provide such a service."

"Very good, Mr Whistler," replied Holmes, "your solution certainly makes sense, and, if true, would equally certainly have an adverse effect on the value of your property. I will look into the matter for you."

Mr Whistler took his leave and Holmes sat puffing his pipe.

"What did you make of our petitioner's matter, good Watson?" asked my friend eventually.

"I confess I would consider it somewhat trivial – indeed at below the level of case that you are used to taking on – were it not that I have an interest in the activities of the Marylebone Coal Supplies business." I explained the announcement I had read in that morning's newspaper, and Holmes listened attentively. I concluded by pointing out that providing ancillary services to its coal supply business was what Marylebone Coal Supplies had stated it wanted to do and that running a fleet of buses would constitute precisely that.

Holmes leant back in his seat

"Well, Watson," he said, "why do you not go down to Houston Close and see what you can make of this business? You have an eye for a commercial opportunity, and this is on your doorstep. If you wish to be an investor, it would be remiss indeed of you not to go down to Houston Close to perform some due diligence on your investment target."

"But I cannot see as far as you, Holmes."

"I have every faith that you will furnish me with the data I require, good Watson. And I confess to a wish for some peace and quiet following our excitement at Winchester."

So it was that that afternoon saw me walking down Houston Close – a tree-lined cul-de-sac with fashionable villas on both sides. At the end of the road stood a high brick wall penetrated by a set of massive and imposing-looking iron gates painted black. A sign above the wall declared that it was the premises of Marylebone Coal Supplies Limited.

I wondered what I could do when, with a grating and a groaning, the gates of the yard opened, and a large coal waggon emerged pulled by four mighty grey geldings straining grimly at their harnesses. I stood back to let the waggon pass and glanced into the yard to be faced with mound after mound of coal. I had little time to see much else as the gates clanged shut. I turned around to see the coal waggon turning right into Marylebone High Street.

I decided I would spend a longer time in Houston Close and thought it as well if I concealed myself to watch the company's activities. Mr Whistler's front-garden had a hedge and, immediately behind it, a mulberry bush, and by squeezing between the two, I was able to see the gate through the hedge while remaining out of sight both of the road and of the house.

Over the next hour or so, the process was repeated again and again. I stood a few minutes more at the gate and watched it open and close to admit coal carriers going in both directions, but, other than to confirm that Marylebone Coal Supplies Limited enjoyed a healthy demand for its product, I was not sure what more there was to do, and I returned to Baker Street to find Holmes sitting at our table. He was surrounded by newspapers opened at the financial pages and in front of him was a note-pad filled with neat columns of numbers in a variety of ink colours.

I gave Holmes an account of my trip to Houston Close which he listened to with the keenest of interest.

"You have performed excellent service, dear Watson. Indeed, your first observations have all but resolved the case in my mind. I congratulate you."

My friend had never said as much to me before, and I was surprised that he should have said as much now. I waited to see if he would caveat his praise in such a way as to turn it into a reproach to my investigative abilities, but none came. Instead, he continued.

"Your insights are indeed of such merit, good Watson, that informed by them I have been able to formulate a plan of action. Be you ready tomorrow night," he added. "We will leave here when it gets dark at half past ten. I cannot tell you at what time we will return. We will need masks, shovels, and dark-lanterns. But we should not light the lanterns till we are at our destination, as I want to minimise the chances of our presence being betrayed to anyone by the smell of hot metal while we are *en route*."

Depending on when this work is read, my reader may be unaware of how scant street lighting was in London in the penultimate decade of the nineteenth century. The main streets around Marylebone were lit by ghostly gas lamps – electric lighting did not come even to a major thoroughfare like the Euston Road until 1897 – and the side roads were completely unlit. A heavy shower was just coming to an end as we reached the junction of Houston Close and Marylebone High Street.

We paused to light our lanterns but kept the glass panes shuttered and put on our masks before proceeding cautiously down the road. When we got to the lofty wall which sealed the premises of Marylebone Coal Supplies, Holmes pressed his lips to my ear.

"Make you a back for me, Watson. I need to climb the wall. When I am at the top, I will pull you up."

Holmes was astride the wall and was reaching down to help me up, when I heard the gates being opened, followed immediately by the rattle of carriages passing through. Was it three or four? I could not be sure – but I heard Holmes utter a quite unwonted oath as he threw back the shutter on the lantern. But, by the time it shone out from the top of the wall, all I could see was the back of a tall vehicle – possibly a horse-omnibus. Trailing this vehicle was, to my complete astonishment, a female hunched over a bicycle who was pedalling hard to keep up. Holmes jumped down from the wall at the same time as I heard the gates slam shut.

"I am a fool! A fool!" he shouted. "I have been outwitted!"

He re-iterated this on our short walk in the darkness back to Baker Street but with the additional comment, "But I will have them yet."

First light on Sunday the thirtieth of June saw Holmes and me back in Houston Close, where Holmes spent considerable time looking for tracks of the vehicles that had passed us the previous night. The shower that had preceded our first visit to Houston Close greatly facilitated this, and Holmes used a tape to measure the width of the carriages, and special paper to make tracings of the wheel marks, and of the horses' hooves. We then returned to Baker Street where he sat all day poring over his library of maps of London.

First thing on Monday morning saw Holmes out of the door. But he returned two hours later with a most downcast expression.

"It's no good Watson. I went to the Land Registry. Railway companies make their money not by transporting passengers but by buying land along the line and using it for housing development. I was wondering whether Marylebone Coal Supplies was going to operate on similar lines by doing some land speculation of its own, but I found no evidence it had taken out another lease." He started pacing our little sitting-room. "I have a case," he said, drawing on his pipe, "but no evidence. Nothing I can put before anyone."

At this moment there was a knock on the door and standing on the threshold stood a woman. Many of the women with whom Holmes had dealings over the years were striking in their beauty, but our petitioner was middle-aged and modestly dressed.

"I am Mary Harris Smith," said she, "and I have a most peculiar matter I want to relate to you."

"Are you connected with the M Harris Smith auditing firm?" I asked.

"I am not connected with the M Harris Smith auditing firm," replied our interlocutor firmly, her chin jutting out.

"My apologies, my dear lady, for my error." I said, concerned that I might have touched on a matter of some sensitivity. "I was reading in the financial press, about the impending flotation of Marylebone Coal Supplies, and noted M Harris Smith was the retiring firm of auditors. When you said your name, I could not help but wonder whether there might be some connection."

"Dr Watson, I would advise you that I do not have a connection with the auditing firm, M Harris Smith. On the contrary, I **am** the auditing firm, M Harris Smith."

In 1889 women were permitted to practise apothecary and medicine in spite of attempts by the British Medical Council to keep these fields closed to women which had had to be overruled by Act of Parliament. But I was not aware that they practised any other profession.

Our petitioner's hand was gloved but I felt it was safe to assume she was married.

I said cautiously, "I take it, dear madame, that you assist your husband in his work by making sure his quills are sharpened, paper is always at hand, post is swiftly opened so that he can deal with it, letters are brought promptly to the mail-box, and the house kept in order so that he can focus on his work. Maybe your skills are so developed that you dabble in dictation and typing as well to assist him."

"No, sir," replied our petitioner, displaying the same firmness in her voice as in her previous remark, "M Harris Smith is my own firm. I took my first bookkeeping classes in 1860 when I was sixteen, and I have worked in accountancy ever since. I set up my own accountancy practice two years ago and have a mixture of clients for auditing and accounting services. I employ seven clerks as well as secretarial staff. I also have some independent hands who provide bookkeeping, auditing, or accounting services as and when needed. My sex is on the rise, and we will not be held back by the weaknesses men impute to us."

Rather to my surprise I saw Holmes smile as though recognising a kindred spirit, and Miss Harris Smith continued.

"Thus, just as your colleague, Mr Holmes, is the world's only consulting detective, so I am its only female accountancy practitioner. It is in connection with this that I would wish to consult with you."

I could see that my colleague was impressed by Miss Harris Smith's self-assurance.

"And how may I help you madame?"

"As your colleague noted, I am the retired auditor of the Marylebone Coal Supplies Company. The owner is a Mr Fastow, who has most ambitious plans for the business. But the business is constricted in growth potential because its premises have limited capacity, its owner is a man without significant capital, and coal is a commodity with many suppliers, so it is hard to make more than a narrow margin on it."

"You make yourself very plain, madame."

"Mr Fastow told me at the time of the last audit that he wanted to sell the business and mentioned a valuation to it which was significantly more than I thought it was worth. At last year's audit I found a number of purchase invoices which had not been booked. I came to the conclusion that the failure to book them had been deliberate. The discovery meant that I had to extend my investigations into the company's affairs, delay the issuance of its accounts, and stand down as its auditor."

"Pray continue."

"When I heard that the business was going to be floated to the public, I was sure that an attempt would be made to inflate the profits. I have accordingly spent much time, both when the business was open and when it was closed, outside the company's premises in Houston Close watching its activities – so monitoring the number of deliveries made to Marylebone Station and listening to discern what I can from over the wall that surrounds the Houston Close site."

"You make yourself very clear."

"In the dead of night on Friday morning I was observing my vigil outside the company's premises, and I noted the delivery of four horse-omnibuses. I knew then that the game was afoot."

I thought Madame Smith was about to start a narrative and leant forward in my seat to hear what happened next.

But she clearly thought she had come to an end – as did Holmes, for he sat back in his seat and blew smoke rings as he often did when he was about to express his thoughts on a client's petition.

Holmes saw my look and said with a smile.

"I think, Madame Smith, I know where this is leading, but perhaps you could explain the matter to my friend."

"The horse-omnibuses were to be concealed under the coal stocks for when the new auditors, Harper Sanderson & Co, conducted their year-end stock count with the quantity surveyors at Houston Close on Saturday the twenty-ninth of June. The day of Friday was spent burying them in coal, and Saturday, the last day of their financial year, was given over to the count at Houston Close."

Miss Harris again paused as though anything else she might say would already be self-evident, but Holmes prompted her with, "And is there anything else you wish to add?"

"Oh yes. During my later audit work on last year's accounts, I became aware that Marylebone Coal Supplies had acquired some premises on a short-term sub-lease in Northolt Park. As a business, that made no sense as a coal merchant needs long-term security of tenure for its activities, which a sub-lease is unlikely to offer them. I could only assume they hired premises in that way so as to ensure that their tenancy would not appear on the land-register."

Again, Miss Harris Smith came to a halt and Holmes had to prompt her to continue her remarks.

"I surmised it was to give them premises to which to move stocks in the night of the twenty-ninth to the thirtieth of June using the horse-buses. Accordingly, it was with my bicycle at the ready that I waited outside their premises on Saturday night. As soon as it got dark, I could hear the horse-omnibuses being retrieved from under the coal. They headed off at about eleven o'clock and I followed them to see them enter the Northolt Park premises. I stayed at Northolt Park and discretely observed the premises until the auditors and the quantity surveyors I had seen arrive at Houston Close on the previous day, arrived at Northolt Park to count the same stock bolstered in quantity by the same horse-buses for a second time."

"And that is your entire narrative?"

There was a pause.

"I do not know that this is relevant to the case, but as I bestrode my bicycle on Saturday night, I was conscious that two men were climbing the wall to the Houston Close site. I did wonder whether someone else might have got wind of the plot I have uncovered and was seeking to find out more."

"Or it may possibly," said my friend with a sidelong glance at me, "have been some pilferers trying to get in to pick coal."

"That strikes me as a most unlikely supposition at the height of summer, even in a June as inclement as this one," said our petitioner, with a look of some disappointment on her face, which made clear her opinion of the plausibility of my colleague's suggestion.

"Perhaps we should continue with our investigation," said Holmes, perhaps a little hastily. "We can form an opinion whether the presence of those two mysterious men becomes more relevant to this matter or whether we can resolve it without explaining their presence."

"Very good, Mr Holmes."

Holmes leant once more back into his seat.

"Yours is a most striking and unusual case, madame, and I must commend you on the insight and dedication you have brought to it. It is rare indeed for a petitioner to come here with not only a case but also a solution. May I ask what it is you want me to do?"

"This morning I went to the headquarters of the Institute of Chartered Accountants at 3 Copthall Buildings to report my concerns. They declined to give me an audience as they stated that my sex meant that my work had no standing with them. I was wondering if you would assist me in completing my investigation and presenting my findings to the Institute."

I could see Holmes wrestling with the dilemma of whether to disclose his own researches into Marylebone Coal Supplies to our client. In the end he confined himself to saying, "Madame, I would advise you that I have my own concerns about this company based on a request from a resident of Houston Close. Accordingly, the good Watson went down to its premises on Saturday afternoon and his immediate observations confirmed your accusation of fraudulent stock accounting."

This was news to me.

"In what way did my observations confirm fraudulent stock accounting?" I asked.

"As you approached the company's premises down Houston Close, you observed mounds of coal in the coal-yard but no horse-omnibuses. That was why I commented on your return that your immediate findings were definitive. You observation of coal but no horse-buses meant that the buses must already have been concealed underneath the coal by the time you saw into the coal-yard on Saturday afternoon. I very much fear however, dear Watson, that the remaining time you spent in Houston Close told me nothing more than that Marylebone Coal Supplies is based in Marylebone and is a supplier of coal – all of which was self-evident before you departed to perform your reconnaissance."

Holmes turned to Miss Harris Smith.

"I have also, dear madame, been carrying out my own desk-based researches into the company. These bear out much of what you say about the company's performance and its prospects." Holmes held up the working papers with their rows of neatly underlined columns and casting ticks in a variety of inks.

He continued.

"I also spent some time at Houston Close yesterday and took tracings of vehicle tracks that had recently egressed the site. With your evidence and mine, madame, we are well armed to further our investigation, and in my view, we would be best served by going to Northolt Park and seeing what we can find out there."

A short train journey from Marylebone saw us out in the countryside at Northolt Park, and Miss Harris Smith directed us to the sublet premises to which she had referred. Like those at Houston Close, these had a lofty wall and a gate, but no one answered the bell when we rang. This disconcerted my friend not in the slightest as he pointed to the roadway leading through to the gate. "The same tracks as we observed emerging from Houston Close," said he, showing us the tracings he had made and the measurements he had taken. "Our case is complete. And the vehicles are entering the site laden – you can see that the tracks they have left are of a depth which means that they were full of coal. There are no shallower tracks indicating an egress."

He stooped in the roadway to take more measurements and make further tracings. "And look, dear madame," he said pointing, "I am even able to confirm the presence of your bicycle with its patched Raleigh tyre." He looked again at the collier's premises. "Such a large site, and yet no activity on a Monday morning. My researches and the more advanced ones of Miss

Harris Smith have progressed on parallel lines and have reached the same outcome."

Another hour saw us back in London, and Holmes's business card was quite sufficient to put us in front of the Institute's grandiosely moustachioed president at the Institute's premises in Tokenhouse Yard.

"What can I do for you, Mr Holmes?" he asked bluffly.

"I have reason," said Holmes, "to believe that a fraud is being committed at Marylebone Coal Supplies Limited. The business is up for sale, and it is their year-end. In the dead of night on the morning of the twenty-eighth of June – so on the early morning of the Friday just past – a number of horse-omnibuses were delivered to their premises in Houston Close near Marylebone Station. On the night of the twenty-ninth of June they moved these vehicles off their site. It is my belief they had been parked under the stocks of coal in their coal-yard for the year-end stock-count attended by their auditors, Harper Sanderson, during the day on the same date. The buses were then filled with coal and taken to a second set of premises and parked under piles of coal there to be counted again on the next day."

"I fear, Mr Holmes," replied the President, "that such matters as you have described are of concern for Marylebone Coal Supplies and their auditors, who will doubtless express their opinion on the accounts of the company in due course. You, by contrast, have no standing here, just as Miss Harris Smith, whose presence I note in your party, has no standing here."

He paused to consider his next words.

"Miss Harris Smith is a trouble-maker," he pronounced, his moustache quivering with anger. "She tried to join the Society of Accountants and Auditors two years ago and was rejected. I suspect she will try her luck here at some point. Any self-respecting president of this Institute will retire if a woman is admitted. Our charter specifically states members must be male."

He paused again and took a large pinch of snuff before continuing.

"I suspect your misguided accusation may be an attempt by her to besmirch the good name of the new auditors, Harper Sanderson & Co, in the hope that this will expedite her admission to our membership. She is already a member of various seditious organizations such as the Parliamentary Committee for Women's Suffrage, the Society for the Return of Women as Poor Law Guardians, the Society for Promoting the Employment of Women, the National Union of Women Workers, the Gentlewoman's Employment Club, and the Soroptimist Club."

"I confess, Mr President," replied Holmes mildly, "that Miss Harris Smith's faculties seem to me at a level that any organization would be proud to have her as a member. I have made my observations about Marylebone Coal Supplies. You have chosen to dismiss them. I will have to consider how to proceed next."

"You have no evidence, Mr Holmes, apart from vehicle tracks, and were not present when the year-end stock count was conducted, so you have no idea what went into the final figures that will form part of the company's accounts."

We were soon back outside, and Miss Harris Smith said she had to return to her office at Bucklesbury while Holmes and I returned to Baker Street where Holmes spent the rest of the day in the deepest contemplation.

The next morning, I perused the newspapers, and my attention was caught by an article in our local paper – the Marylebone Gazette.

Under the headline, "New role for local entrepreneur" was a piece about the sale of the Marylebone Coal Supplies company, and an interview with the man who was described as its former proprietor, Mr Andrew Fastow. He had made a private sale of the business.

"I felt, in the end," he was quoted as saying, "that I had taken the business Marylebone Coal Supplies as far as I could and needed a new challenge. I had originally intended a flotation to obtain outside capital, but I received an offer that was as much I could have netted in a public sale. Accordingly, I have handed on the baton to that experienced supplier of fuel consumables, Messrs Skilling, MacEnron, & Ley Limited, who, I am sure will be able to take the business forward at a rapid rate."

The former owner of the Marylebone Coal Supplies Company, the newspaper added, had secured an appointment as the small business and ethics adviser at the well-known, Ascent Sure Limited – the business advisers associated with but independent of the Harper Sanderson & Co auditing firm. Mr Fastow was quoted as saying, "I look forward to my new role at the aptly named Ascent Sure Limited with great excitement. I am flattered that it should be felt that my experience and insight into running a small business would be of benefit to other small businesses. I can't wait to start."

Holmes threw the newspaper to the floor when I showed him the article. "Not only has justice been thwarted," said he, drawing heavily on his pipe, "but the perpetrators of falsehood have been rewarded."

All day he sat smoking the black tobacco he consumed when in his darkest moods, and I feared what substance he might turn to next. But at just after six o'clock there was a knock on the door, and we were joined by Miss Harris Smith.

"I wanted," said she, "to thank you for your help in my investigation."

"I am sorry," replied my friend, "that I was unable to bring it to a more satisfactory conclusion."

"I note from my review of the press that the matter has already found its own resolution, and I would now wish to focus on serving my clients rather than conducting independent investigations of my own," countered she. "I also felt that you, Mr Holmes, showed a remarkable talent for financial investigation and wondered whether you might be able to carry out investigative assignments on my behalf, although I fear," she said, turning to me, "that such investigations could not be the subject of a published account as I scrupulously observe client confidentiality. But such work would be remunerated," she added, looking back at Holmes.

So it was that Holmes carried out financial investigations as a consulting advisor when his other case work allowed. The financial rewards this brought enabled him to maintain a certain style even when his detective consultancy work brought scant monetary rewards. I think the exhilaration generated by finding solutions to financial matters also gave Holmes the mental equilibrium he needed to render unattractive the exhilaration offered by his seven-per-cent solution of cocaine. Certainly, his interest in the needle dwindled to almost nothing after he started working with M Harris Smith.

For her own part Miss Harris Smith continued to lobby for membership of the Institute without success. It took until the passing of the Sex Disqualification (Removal) Act in 1919 before she was finally admitted as the Institute's first female member.

Holmes decided he would benefit from the academic rigour of the Institute's entry examination, but, although he passed its course of entry with ease, he declined to apply for membership until Miss Harris Smith had been granted it. By the time this had happened in 1920 – the same time as women were allowed to practise as lawyers for the first time – Holmes had already withdrawn to his bee-keeper's cottage on the South Downs so the Institute's records remain unable to claim him as an alumnus.

But in *The Stockbroker's Clerk* he introduced himself to a potential employer as an accountant called Mr Harris, and I cannot imagine he would have done this had he not had his association with the remarkable Miss Mary Harris Smith.

M Harris Smith – Afterword

The biography of Mary Harris Smith presented here (she is pictured on the cover in the top row to the right of Dante Gabriel Rossetti), is accurate.

2020 marked one hundred years since her elevation as the first woman member of the UK's Institute of Chartered Accountants making her the British equivalent of a United States Certified Public Accountant or CPA. She had been trying to obtain membership for many decades and the response she got for repeated applications is replicated in Dr Watson's account of events.

It cannot be a coincidence that Sherlock Holmes referred to himself as an accountant called Mr Harris in *The Stockbroker's Clerk*, and it must be assumed that Sherlock Holmes and Mary Harris Smith had a close association which is revealed here for the first time.

Dr Watson's account is remarkable in that it appears to foretell future events as well as telling of historical events. The characters in M Harris Smith apart from Holmes, Watson, Harris Smith, and Holmes's petitioner, Grant Whistler, all have names associated with the Enron Scandal of the first decade of the twenty-first century.

One of the delights of walking round London is to see plaques dedicated to famous men and in, all too few cases, women who are associated with the site where the plaque is mounted. In 2020, a plaque was set up near the site of Mary Harris Smith's office although her connection with Sherlock Holmes had not been revealed at that point so Holmes's connection to the site is not mentioned.

A picture of this plaque is below.

A Story with a Health-Warning

Much ink has been spilt over what my friend Mr Sherlock Holmes might have been doing in the three years between May 1891 and April 1894 which his many followers are increasingly referring to as the Great Hiatus. At the time of the story titled *The Empty House*, he told me of his exploits as a Norwegian explorer under the adopted name of Sigerson, of visits to Mecca and Khartoum, as well as of experiments on coal-tar derivatives conducted in Montpellier, although it was clear that this was not an exhaustive list.

By contrast, little attention has been paid to what I might have been doing at this time although the same story also referred to the death of my dear wife, Mary Morstan. I do not wish to dwell here on the details of her final affliction save to say that it was lingering, painful, and borne with typical fortitude, but rather to focus on the affect it had on my own financial situation.

My reader may have assumed that as a medical practitioner, I would have been the person to minister to my wife's needs. But, like many of my fellow doctors, I was reluctant to treat someone of my own family myself, and in any case, as someone with a military background, I felt unqualified to intervene in her condition. And in the final stages of her illness, I was so distracted as to be unable to give my professional work the attention that running a medical practice requires. Thus, my financial position deteriorated as I was forced to seek treatment for her from other physicians. Bills for their fees mounted up alarmingly at the same time as my own income had sharply diminished.

So it was that after Mary's departure from this life, I found myself in my study in December 1893 after the last of that day's paltry count of patients had left, looking gloomily down at the lengthy list of pressing calls on my purse.

"There is a caller for you, sir," said the maid from outside my study.

"I have no wish to be disturbed," countered I, but it was too late for a small twinkly-eyed man with a thick head of silvery hair was already in the room.

"Dr Watson," said he. "It is good of you to have given me an audience for I am sure you have many other calls on your time."

"I fear," I grunted in a not over-friendly tone, "that my practice is not very engaging at the best of times. And this," I added, glancing briefly down at the list of outstanding bills and then at the largely empty appointments book for the following day beside it, "is in no sense the best of times."

"Then, dear doctor," breezed my interlocuter, "my arrival here may be apposite. I have come here to ask you if you would be interested in augmenting your income in a way which is remunerative, trivial, well-suited to your personal qualities, and entirely without risk to you."

Experience had taught me that if a proposition sounds too good to be true, it probably is, but I felt that this was no time to pass up a such an attractive opportunity, and, borrowing one of Holmes's favourite expressions for eliciting information, I responded with, "Pray continue."

"My name is Evan Peterson, and I was, until recently, the member of parliament for a north-west English constituency."

"Your name is of-course known to me although I recall you were required to stand down from parliament with your reputation under, if I may say so, something of a cloud. The precise details of your fall from grace I fear I no longer remember."

"Alas, that is so. I had been informing government ministers of potential suppliers of specialist food products."

"That does not seem to me to be a reason to be forced to give up your position as a member of parliament," I grunted again, wondering where this was leading. "Presumably the supplier of specialist food products was based in your constituency, so you were only helping your constituents."

"As a public figure, I see it as one's duty to help ones.." he broke off as though not sure of how exactly to express himself and, and then continued, "one's country in any way that one can, and providing what I regard as a brokering service – effectively putting a demand in contact with a supply – is the best way to do so."

My reader will, I fear, have to decide whether I have punctuated the above paragraph correctly as I remain unsure whether the first 'ones' should have an apostrophe to indicate the meaning Mr Peterson eventually came out with, or whether his initial thought was that it was one's duty to help oneself – so, without an apostrophe, as I have rendered it.

Mr Peterson continued.

"You are a man of the world, dear Doctor, and can see the broader picture. But some people, I regret, formed a most narrow-minded opinion of what represents appropriate arrangements in these circumstances. The fact that I secured a major contract with the government for a client on a supply that no one else was allowed to bid for, was seen in less well-informed circles as inappropriate for a member of parliament. And the same unkind people took a dim view of the thousand guineas – a mere trifle for the value of what I delivered to the nation – that I took for providing my help."

"A thousand guineas!" I expostulated, glancing down again at the list of my outstanding debts, and reflecting that such a sum was not far off a year of my fees in normal times.

"Preposterously small, I agree," said Mr Peterson with a wistful sigh.

He waited, as though expecting me to say something, but then continued.

"You will of-course understand that a man of my talents could earn many times that if I took on all the opportunities which come my way without displaying any sort of scruples," Peterson shrugged and then went on. "But, like you, I regarded a thousand guineas as some slight recompense for forgoing some of the more succulent opportunities that being a member of parliament precluded me from taking. And I feel that broadening my knowledge was of benefit to my constituents."

"So the fee you took was to enable you to broaden your own knowledge rather than putting your existing knowledge at the service of your paymaster?" I asked in some wonder.

"I would, of-course, good Doctor, quite understand if so meagre a sum as one thousand guineas per annum were, perhaps, not of any interest to you," replied Mr Peterson, ignoring my question, "but the requirements of you, if you would care to listen to the proposition I have, would indeed be almost negligible."

"Pray continue," I said again, still doing my best not to appear to be too interested, for what my caller was saying seemed intriguing but unworthy of being taken seriously.

"The apothecary manufacturers produce a stream of new products but in the fever of their inventiveness, they find it difficult to attract attention to them in a way that leads to sales."

"And what do you see as my role in this?"

"Dear Doctor, through your writings you are the best-known medical practitioner in the country. And your name is a watchword for all that is good and decent. You would be commissioned to do no more than to draw the attention of your brother-physics to the latest preparations, so that they could prescribe them to their patients. Your fellow medicos will believe your word on the efficacy of the preparations where they might not believe the blandishments of the representatives of the manufacturers of those preparations."

"Do you have a list of the sorts of products you would like me to recommend?" I rejoindered slightly warily, as I was aware that I had not been as abreast as I should have been of the latest advances in medical science – indeed, as I said this, I cast a furtive glance into a corner of my study where a pile of papers and circulars about new medical preparations lay dustily unread.

Peterson handed over a list – it was a relief not to be looking at a list of my debts – but I saw an immediate problem as I scanned it. "I fear I know nothing at all about Jervis's Hair Restorer, Smythe's Slimming Tablets, or Girtin's Sovereign Backrub, and, accordingly, I would be most reluctant to endorse them."

"My dear Doctor, how much do you think a man in my position knows about specialist food processing? That is why it is of such benefit to all that I should receive an incentive to increase my knowledge. As a member of parliament, I regarded myself both as an obedient servant of the people of my constituency, and as a hansom-cab available for hire to all. Now I am merely the latter. But I have the same name as I had when I persuaded a government minister who had previously been in pupillage in my barrister's chambers to award the contract to which I referred. And I am sure that your name will be just as effective in generating sales for the list of products you have before you with your brother-doctors. You may fit in your sales activity at any time your medical practice allows."

"And what do you seek in return?"

"My only requirement is that you pass to me a tenth of the commission you will make from the manufacturers of these preparations. There is thus no risk at all to you in this."

We discussed matters to and fro for a while but ended up settling very much on the terms stated above.

I soon found my time filled in a way that was far more profitable than sitting in my practice waiting for patients to arrive and then wating for them to settle their bills as the medical companies paid me a commission each time a brother-doctor undertook to prescribe one of their preparations. My reader may have wondered what I was doing in Park Lane on the weekday afternoon in April 1894 when I collided with a hunch-backed bibliophile who turned out to be a disguised Sherlock Holmes. I confess here that I was in fact on my way from the quarters I then occupied in Kensington to Harley Street where I was to peddle some new preparations to the many doctors who had their practices there.

To my relief, the doctors I saw agreed to prescribe the products which I was drawing to their attention and raised no questions either about their efficacy or about the propriety of my making the recommendation. This relief was, I confess, as naught compared to that that I felt as I made a start in clearing my debts.

I had been engaged in this business for not so very long when the smooth Mr Peterson called again.

"I have a commission for you that is slightly out of the ordinary," he said. "I have received a request from the Distillers' Association to represent them with a government minister tomorrow."

"And who are Distillers' Association?" asked I in some wonder.

"There are three big distillers in the country whose sales represent quite nine tenths of the market. Although they compete fiercely against each other, they recognise that they have common interests, and they use the Distillers' Association to represent them before the government and other regulatory authorities."

"And what has that to do with me?"

"The minister we are seeing is a Mr Self, whose ministerial portfolio is this country's health. I cannot doubt that it is a matter related to health that he wants to see us about – hence my interest in engaging a doctor to accompany me."

I spoke only to confirm that this was indeed a commission quite out of the run of what I had been doing up until then and there was a long pause as each of us waited for the other to speak.

"What is the price you are seeking, Dr Watson?" asked Mr Peterson at last.

"One hundred guineas," I suggested, much more in hope than in expectation.

"Done!" said he, and so it was that on the morrow I found myself sitting alongside Mr Peterson and facing the sober-looking government minister, Mr Self.

"We in the government are very worried about the level of consumption of alcoholic beverages particularly among poor people. Such drinks are addictive and deleterious to health," said he.

"Taken in moderation," replied Mr Peterson, "such drinks are a source of enjoyment to the consumers' tongue, a purgative to their systems, and a means of engendering bonhomie in company. Extensive research among consumers indicates that very few people over-indulge to the extent that have the consequences you refer to."

"We would," continued Mr Self, paying no heed to the objection, "like to introduce a program of labelling for drinks with a high alcohol content warning people of the dangers such drinks pose."

"It is iniquitous," objected Mr Peterson, "for the government to single out the industry I represent for what I can only describe as interference. What you are proposing will drive up costs and the industry will be compelled to pass those higher costs onto consumers. The likeliest result of what you suggest is that poor people will take to distilling their own drinks which will then not be produced under controlled conditions, and so are likely to cause far more harm to their health than anything that our products cause. Or they will smuggle in spirits from overseas, depriving the Exchequer of revenues and putting supply into the hands of criminal gangs."

My own experience of advocating medicinal products to brother-physics had not provided me with any remedy about which I held any strong feelings, but this ministerial proposal I construed as an attack on my profession.

"Minister," I said, "speaking as a medical man, I am appalled at what is being suggested. If you have had the chance to read any of my works, you will see that a tot of a spirit is the main medical treatment that I administer. It blunts pain in the patient, it kills the causes of illness, and it facilitates the rapid elimination of those causes of illness from the body."

I do not think Mr Self had been expecting one of the representatives of the Distillers' Association to be a doctor. There was a silence as he thought about a response, and I continued, warming to my theme.

"The doctor's battery of remedies is limited enough already without making them more expensive. When a child does not thrive, I recommend sweets such as humbugs or sherbet as a treat to encourage clearance of the dinner-plate. When a patient presents himself to me with an impediment to breathing, I recommend increased consumption of tobacco. And when a patient has any failing of the stomach, I prescribe regular doses of brandy. You would surely not consider applying health warnings to sweets or to tobacco products, and there is thus no argument for applying health warnings to distilled spirits either. I am sure, that for every person who over-indulges in them to the detriment of their health, there are ten people whose health benefits from their consumption."

Mr Self seemed taken aback by these arguments.

"I will commission an inter-departmental committee to investigate the advantages and disadvantages of the proposal," he said at last.

"It always pays to present multiple arguments as it throws uncertainty into the minister's mind. That is why he is going to set up a committee consisting of representatives from different government ministries," observed Mr Peterson drily, as we emerged into Whitehall. "Committees made up like that take minutes, sit for years,…and never reach a conclusion."

He pressed what I found afterwards to be a cheque for one hundred guineas into my hand, exclaiming, "An excellent result, dear Doctor! It is my considered view that an attack on our industry delayed, is an attack on our industry forestalled. I cannot imagine that today could have gone any better."

When Holmes returned to London after his long absence, and I reverted to living once more in Baker Street, I continued with my business of advising my brother-doctors of the availability of new medical products which occupied much of my energies. I refrained from telling Holmes about it as I still felt a certain disquiet about taking money for endorsing preparations I knew very little about.

By contrast, in spite of his unparalleled investigative skill which I had done so much to advertise, cases for Holmes were thin in the first few months on his return – indeed I quote my friend's plaints at how unenterprising the London criminal class had become at the opening of *The Norwood Builder*. As I had previously set out in *The Empty House,* Holmes expressed the wish not to be associated with the capture of Sebastian Moran, the murderer of Ronald Adair, and so was not mentioned in the press coverage of the arrest or in the subsequent trial. The suppression of Holmes's involvement in the latter case may have delayed the arrival of new clients as my friend's return, while not a secret, was not a topic of general discussion.

"Alas," as Holmes put it to me one day, "the equity you built up in my name as an investigator has been quite dissipated as other detectives have been able to bruit their services in my absence." Time for me hung heavy too as, if running a medical practice had left me far from being fully engaged, my reader may imagine how much less of my time was engaged in providing Holmes with help on the few cases that came our way.

On the evening of Tuesday the fourteenth of May 1895 Holmes stood slightly forlorn at the window of our little sitting-room as he scanned passers-by for a potential client.

"Finally," said he with a chuckle. I rose from my chair, and he turned to me with a look of triumph on his face.

"I think I recognise those symptoms. I see, good Watson, a well-dressed man coming hesitatingly up the street from the Metropolitan Line Railway station, and I observe that he is checking the street numbers. He walks with a limp and has a new walking stick. This suggests that he has recently sought medical intervention, but he will not be seeking to do so here in Baker Street when Harley Street is around the corner. Thus, it is hard to imagine that he has any other purpose in looking at the street numbers than to come here to seek my advice. It is re-assuring to know that age has not withered my powers of deduction or my ability to attract clients."

My friend sat down in his chair by the fire and rubbed his hands in anticipation. But the minutes passed and no ring on the door came.

"That might have constituted your briefest ever case, Holmes," quipped I, but barely were the words out of my mouth when a ring on the bell finally came followed by the sound of footsteps on the stairs.

"Mr Arthur Arnold!" announced the boy in buttons, and Holmes was soon ushering our petitioner into the chair beside the window.

He sat in silence for some time, looking first at me and then at Homes as though still unsure on whether he really wanted to consult.

"I thought you were no more," he said to Holmes at last. "I read Dr Watson's account of your demise, but his report, if I may say so, seems to have been somewhat exaggerated."

"My client, dear Doctor," interjected Holmes confidently, ignoring Mr Arnold's astonishment, "has a matter to present but is not sure whether it is an appropriate one to raise or whether I am the right person to raise it with. Otherwise, he would not have walked up from the station to the door and then gone past it, before doubling back after he had made a final decision that he would indeed consult. He is a man of means – only a man of means would have both a pink Financial Times and a white Financial News under his arm – though I note from the condition of the paper of both that he has not taken the trouble to read either. Judging by his bejewelled and monogrammed cufflinks, I would surmise that my petitioner has ascended right to the top of the corporate tree, and, as he has come to consult with me at the end of the working day rather than straight from his home, that it is a business matter rather than a private one on which would wish to consult."

Our client stared at Holmes in some wonderment.

"You are largely right in your comments, Mr Holmes."

"Only largely?" asked Holmes, eye-brows slightly raised.

"You are right to infer that I have severe doubts on whether I should raise the matter on my mind with anyone, and if so with whom. And I confess I carry the output of the financial press as a matter of duty rather than as something I would actually wish to read. It is like wearing a uniform – thus, much like the cufflinks to which you refer. And I am the managing director of

Amalgamated Consumer Spirits, so your deduction that I have ascended to the top of the barrel in the corporate world is also accurate."

"I think, Mr Arnold," responded Holmes with some asperity, "it is fair to say that I was rather more than just largely right with my observations".

"Your observations on me, Mr Holmes, are accurate as far as they go. But the matter on which I would wish to consult on is something I would wish to raise with your companion, Dr Watson. As I have stated, I had no idea you were still alive, and I only called here to get a forwarding address for your colleague, as it was to him that I wanted to address my disquisition. Dr Watson's address when he lived here is of course well known, whereas the address he moved to after leaving Baker Street is not. It is indeed a matter of great good fortune to find him here thus obviating the need to go to a further address to present my petition."

I had never before seen my friend look in any way crestfallen, but I can think of no other adjective to describe how he looked now.

"And having found reports of my death somewhat exaggerated, do you not now wish to avail yourself of my skills?" he asked, a slight note of pleading in his voice.

Mr Arnold paused for a moment and then responded.

"When I read Dr Watson's eloquent account of the matter he described as *The Final Problem*, I thought your conduct of the case left much to be desired, Mr Holmes. You fled to the Continent at the *moment critique* of your investigation, your desire to have your friend's company on your flight put him into unnecessary danger, and you then allowed yourself to be lured into meeting Professor Moriarty *à deux*, which could only serve his purposes, and could never serve yours. You could have had the full force of the law behind you had you chosen to have it."

Holmes was for once lost for a response and Arnold continued.

"For my part, I have an imminent appointment with the government minister responsible for this nation's health. I happened to mention this to my own doctor this morning when I went to see him on a routine matter, and he recommended Dr Watson to me as the man who had drawn his attention to the excellent Pyne's Universal Remedy. My doctor knows Dr Watson as a man with an understanding of medical matters and of the ways of the world. He also commented on Dr Watson's powers of advocacy for the products he recommends, which suggests to me he might be the person to make a case against whatever attack on my company's business the minister proposes – for a summons to see a government minister normally has no other objective."

Back in the early 1880s when Holmes and I first shared quarters in Baker Street, it was not unknown for him to beg sole use of the sitting-room from me so that clients could consult with him confidentially, but this was the first time that it was I who asked him for the room's sole use. Chagrin was written on his face as Holmes eventually withdrew to his room, and Mr Arnold explained himself.

"As I stated when your colleague was here," began Mr Arnold. "I have received a summons to attend a meeting with a government minister, Mr Self, in Whitehall. A summons of this type is the lot of a managing director who needs to be adept, among other things, at marketing, finance, production, logistics, sales, and public relations. I know not for what reason the summons has been issued but I do know that I have no choice other than to attend."

"Mr Self, of-course, I know personally," I responded cautiously, though I declined to disclose how I was acquainted with him, "but," I continued, "I would have thought that dealing with the government was handled by your industry's trade association."

"I am surprised both that you know Mr Self personally and that you know about the Distillers' Association," replied Mr Arnold, "but such specialist industry knowledge on your part merely confirms the wisdom of my choice of you as advocate. You are right to say that such matters would previously have been dealt with by the association which had been set up by ourselves and our competitors, British Spirits, and Classic Whiskies to represent our common interests. But Classic Whiskies has a new managing director, a Mr Canning, who has the wildest ideas of how to run a business. His company withdrew support for the association, so each company now represents itself. I expect we will find that Mr Canning, and the managing director of British Spirits, Mr Byers, have received the same summons, and so will attend tomorrow's meeting as well."

He rose to leave but I coughed discretely, and said, "I fear, Mr Arnold, that I cannot provide my advocacy services unremunerated even for a cause as worthy as yours."

Eventually we agreed a fee of one-hundred-and-fifty guineas and the next week found Mr Arnold and me in the atrium of the ministry.

I was unsurprised when Mr Arnold introduced me to Messrs Byers and Canning, the first carrying the financial press with him as a decoration rather than as something to read just as Mr Arnold did, and the second, a much younger man with a rakish expression. I was much more surprised to see in the company of Mr Byers was Mr Self while Mr Canning was accompanied by none other than Mr Peterson.

"My appointment as minister was terminated last week, but I was offered a senior position as a consultant by British Spirits which more than recompenses me for the loss of my post," said Mr Self, as though in explanation of his new role.

"I think I mentioned to you, Dr Watson, that my powers of advocacy were like a hansom-cab," chimed in Mr Peterson in turn. "I am available to hire by anyone who chooses. Classic Whiskies has sought my advocacy, and I in turn am happy to provide it."

We were soon before the new minister, the tall and serious-looking Mr Turgiss, who opened proceedings by expressing the same concerns about the consumption of spirits that Mr Self had expressed when he had been a minister. I was reassured when Mr Self, representing British Spirits, responded to him using the same arguments that I had made previously. Mr Arnold, Mr Byers, and I all supported him in his submissions.

Mr Turgiss then asked Classic Whiskies in the persons of Mr Canning and Mr Peterson for their views.

"Clearly, Minister," responded Mr Peterson earnestly, "as a company, Classic Whiskies does not want its products to be consumed to excess by anyone. If you feel that a system of labelling spirits would assist in warning people of the dangers of excess consumption, then we will have no choice but to label them to advise our consumers of the risks. Perhaps your department would like to come up with a proposal for a text, and we will seek to implement what you ask for."

Everyone in the room, apart from Mr Canning of Classic Whiskies, looked in some wonder at Mr Peterson who was expressing views so different from what he had advocated previously.

"I cannot help but agree with my colleague, Mr Peterson," added Mr Canning soberly, "and indeed, I think we should seek to go further. A single warning on our bottles would, after an initial frisson of excitement, soon cease to have an effect. It would become like wallpaper and so have no effect on consumption. I would suggest that the health labels need to be more impactful. I would propose that there be a selection of perhaps six health warnings highlighting the impact of drink on different parts of the body so that the consumer gets a message on health which is consistent in its general import but varied in the specific aspect of health it targets."

"So, you are arguing for even greater complexity in the production process than that being proposed by the minister," Mr Byers remonstrated with Mr Canning. "That will drive up the distillers' costs and make some products unviable. We will have cut back on investment and reduce our count of hired hands which will hit areas where there are not many hirers of labour."

149

"I am seeking a way of addressing the minister's concerns about public health," replied Mr Canning with a most injured look on his face. "There is no point in any of us being here if that is not our objective."

"Do you have any other suggestions, Mr Canning?" asked Mr Turgiss.

"We should also look to raise the tax on whisky. At present it is levied at a percentage of the retail price and paid by the retailer. It would make much more sense if it were a tax paid by the manufacturer on supply to the wholesaler and that it be a specific amount per bottle based on a percentage of the most popular brand."

"Anything else?"

"And we should ban advertising of distilled spirits so that they do not achieve too wide an appeal."

"So, to summarise," said Mr Turgiss, "To address the government's concerns about public health, Classic Whiskies would like health warnings on the bottles, higher taxes, and a ban on advertising. By contrast, Amalgamated Consumer Spirits and British Spirits, while sharing these concerns, wish to do nothing"

The nods from around the table at Mr Turgiss's summary constituted the only point on which the meeting's attendees agreed.

"I shall discuss your submissions with the prime minister," said Mr Turgiss.

We emerged from the ministry into Whitehall and waited in line for hansom-cabs.

I noticed Mr Canning blinking, and I asked him if he had something in his eye. "Only a gleam," replied he enigmatically, and disappeared into a hansom-cab with Mr Peterson without saying another word.

As Mr Arnold, Mr Byers, Mr Self, and I waited in a line for hansom-cabs of our own, Mr Arnold turned to me and said, "I fear a more analytical approach might have delivered better results. Maybe I should have involved your friend, Mr Holmes, after all. I fear Dr Watson, I fail to see how your advocacy today has been of any value."

I took this comment about the apparent failure of our representations as a hint that Mr Arnold might seek to withhold my honorarium and replied, perhaps slightly heatedly, "It is unlikely that Mr Holmes would accept a commission if there were any matters outstanding between you and me."

We stood facing each other.

"You are expecting me to pay for your advocacy even though it appears that the government will impose severe restrictions on our industry?"

"If you commission a barrister for his services," replied I, "you expect to pay his fee. Whether you win the case or not."

We stood in Whitehall glowering for some time. I would hesitate to say voices were raised but Mr Byers and Mr Self had long since disappeared before Mr Arnold finally blinked and agreed to ensure my fee was paid.

A cab finally arrived, we drove to Baker Street, and headed up the stairs to see Holmes.

It was to the consternation of Mr Arnold and me when we entered the sitting-room to find Mr Byers of British Spirits in the chair Holmes normally asks clients to sit in.

"I am not at all sure of the propriety of this!" said both Mr Arnold and Mr Byers when they saw each other. "Come gentlemen," said Holmes, "you have a common interest to see this matter resolved. Pray consult. Mr Byers, perhaps you would like to speak on behalf of both yourself and Mr Arnold of the events of today and I will provide you with an explanation of what is happening."

"You seem very confident," said both Mr Arnold and Mr Byers again in unison.

"I can see no further than you gentlemen but my cases involving big business have solutions that are obvious to anyone except perhaps to those charged with the running of big businesses," said Holmes with a smile. "Although," he added as an afterthought, "I will have to make one trivial enquiry to confirm my conclusions."

Between them Mr Arnold and Mr Byers set out the events of the afternoon.

Mr Byers concluded his account with the comment, "Classic Whiskies' position would be disastrous for the industry. Complex health warnings on spirit bottles and higher taxes will reduce demand for distilled spirits which will increase our unit costs as the same fixed costs will be spread over fewer bottles."

"Indeed," concurred Mr Arnold. "And just as Classic Whiskies' position makes no sense for the industry, it makes even less sense to them as an individual business. The company has but one product in its portfolio – Ronnie Talker. That is, by a distance, the leading spirit in the country and attracts a premium price even though it is no different from what we make. Classic Whiskies advertises Ronnie Talker heavily, so why would they want a ban on advertising? By contrast Amalgamated and British Spirits both have a wide portfolio of lower-priced products which have a localised following but nationwide none attracts more than a small per centage of total consumption."

"Mr Holmes," added Mr Byers in some agitation, "as a result of this attack on our industry, we will have to make major cuts in our business. We will have to close distilleries and bottling plants. As a first step to doing this I telegrammed the landlord of one of our bonded warehouses saying we wanted to terminate our contract forthwith. I was astonished when no sooner had I sent it when a telegram arrived back from the landlord saying that Classic Whiskies had been in touch to seek more space and so he would release us from our rental agreement even though we were in breach of contract. I had heard, Mr Holmes," here he broke off to give a sly glance at Mr Arnold, "that you were back in London, and it was an obvious step to hasten hither to see you."

"I fear Mr Holmes," said Mr Arnold, "that it may be my duty to approach the stock exchange to advise them that young Mr Canning has taken leave of his senses and that trade in his company's shares should be suspended."

"Most stimulating!" exclaimed Holmes. "I will not even need to make the trivial investigations that I thought would be necessary."

He paused and lit his pipe.

"So, are you telling me that the opportunity being offered by the changes in legislation has not occurred you?"

"The changes proposed offer no opportunities at all."

"So, what is your explanation for Mr Canning's behaviour besides insanity?"

"He has acquired an unreasoning hatred of the spirits industry and wants to destroy it," speculated Mr Arnold.

"He is looking to curry favour with the government perhaps in the hope of getting an advisory position," hazarded Mr Byers, "or maybe a knighthood."

"Or both," added Mr Arnold.

There was a pause before Mr Arnold and Mr Byers chimed,

"We really came to get an explanation from you, Mr Holmes, not to provide an explanation ourselves."

Holmes drew again on his pipe.

"You say you that the three companies have nine-tenths of the market. What about the other tenth?" he asked.

"They are all small suppliers with a highly localised demand."

"So their business will become unviable with the increased complexity of manufacturing? Where do you think the demand for their product will go? I would have thought the likeliest beneficiary is Ronnie Talker as, from what you say, it is the best-known product."

Silence.

"And you do not see that with only a few products, it will be easy for Classic Whiskies to accommodate complex labelling, and that both your companies will find short production runs unprofitable, and so you will have to discontinue minor lines. And consumers of those too will seek new products. It is hard to see how the market leading product cannot benefit from that."

"And the ban on advertising? How will that help a company that advertises its products heavily?"

"When the ban comes, Classic will be unable to advertise its products. But nobody else will be able to advertise their products either. Thus, the proportion of the market each supplier provides will be frozen but the cost of sustaining those shares will largely disappear. There will always be a demand for whisky and the advertising each of you pays is a fight over the proportion of drinkers each product attracts and not a fight about getting new consumers to start drinking whisky. The only requirement for the business will be making sure that its products remain in stock. And again, whom do you think that will help? Companies with a portfolio of niche products with a small and often localised market share such as yours, or a company with a small number of market leading products such as Classic Whiskies?"

"But surely the demand for whisky will contract if there are health warnings on bottles."

"The effect of strong drinks on health has been known for centuries without number. I hardly think an additional piece of labelling will make any difference to the demand."

"And the higher rate of tax? How can that help Classic?"

"My dear sir, what is the easiest way to gain an initial foothold with a new product?"

"To sell it cheap of course."

"And if tax on whisky is a proportion of the retail price, who really pays the tax on a low-price product?"

"All our products are properly taxed," said both business leaders.

"But the difference in tax on a low-priced compared to a high-priced product is paid by the government as it foregoes the tax that would be paid on a higher priced product. And if the tax is a specific amount per bottle based on a proportion of the tax on a premium product, it is much less profitable to launch a product at a low price as a high fixed cost will still have to be covered. And you will not be able to advertise it to make consumers aware of the existence of your new product."

"And why are Classic acquiring extra warehousing space?"

"What are you going to do in response to the measures taken?"

"We will cut all costs and empty our stores to get product into retailers with the old labelling and the current system of taxation which is borne by retailers."

"And does it not occur to you to pay the current tax on the retailers' behalf before the goods leave your warehouse?"

"Why would we want to do that?"

"That way you can sell your whisky with the old tax at the new higher price."

There was a silence as it dawned on Mr Byers and Mr Arnold that the new market conditions for whisky offered unchanged consumption, ruin for competing small manufacturers, and a windfall margin opportunity. And, that by contrast with Classic Whiskies, they were ill-placed to take advantage of that opportunity.

"So what do you suggest we should do?" they asked wanly.

"Our bonuses are tied to our profits," added Mr Byers.

"And to our share-price," intoned Mr Arnold dolefully.

"If what is proposed passes, both our profits and our share-price will fall compared to Classic," chimed in Mr Byers.

"In that case, gentlemen," responded Holmes briskly, "you might like both to consider buying shares in Classic Whiskies."

"We cannot do that. We must find a way of forestalling the government's plans."

My friend turned to me.

"I fear, good Watson," said Holmes, a familiar twinkle in his eye, "I may be implicating you with insider knowledge on future movements in share-prices if I make you party to my suggestion on how Mr Byers and Mr Arnold may redeem their situation. Would you mind if I had private use of this, our shared sitting-room?"

And that was the last I heard from the spirits industry.

My readers may feel that ending this account of events here short-changes them by not giving a solution as I candidly do not know what Holmes recommended to Mr Byers and Mr Arnold at this point.

But in the weeks that followed I received numerous approaches from leading figures in the tobacco and confectionary industries worried about rumours of government plans for new packaging requirements for their products, limitations on how and when they could advertise, and increases in taxes on their products. I subsequently represented them in front of numerous governmental committee meetings at a charge-out rate well above the one-hundred-and fifty guineas charge I had made to Mr Arnold. The committees struggled earnestly with the conflicting priorities of public health, personal freedom, local employment prospects, and tax raising. I also noted that the tobacco companies seemed remarkably well-informed on the latest research on the properties of coal-tar derivatives, and I cannot help but wonder whether Holmes was feeding them his findings from Montpellier to supplement his income although he gave me no information on the matter.

After I (and many others) had made our submissions, the government announced that the deadline for completing a wide-ranging review of the packaging and taxation of tobacco, alcoholic beverages, and confectionery had been extended, and that the matter would be the subject of a review by a quasi-autonomous non-governmental organization.

This review is to be headed by none other than Mr Peterson.

In the announcement to this effect, the minister justly described Mr Peterson as a man who can see all sides of every argument. The minister who made the announcement was a Mr Bland, the successor of Mr Turgiss, who had left the government to become an advocate for a number of trade associations in which capacity he, Mr Self, and I often encountered each other while making our submissions.

For my part, I cannot fail to see the hand of my friend in getting objections to the proposed measures from so many sources, and I will be surprised if their implementation is not delayed for the foreseeable future.

A Story with a Health-Warning – Afterword

It is often assumed that big companies are competitive in tooth and claw, constantly seeking to put each other out of business.

This account of events, by contrast, reveals how big businesses deliberately seek complex regulation to keep small and low-priced competitors out. This is why almost all the drinks, tobacco, and confectionery products we buy are sold by a few hugely profitable multi-national giants as only they can afford to meet government product requirements. The man pictured on the front cover to the right of William of Orange is the original man behind the world's best-known Scottish whisky brand. There is no suggestion that the behaviour of Classic Whiskies in this account of events from well over one hundred years ago was in any way criminal. It is merely self-serving for the big manufacturers. But it should be remembered that serving the interests of their shareholders is precisely the duty of leaders of big companies.

Just as the events described in *M Harris Smith* seems to foreshadow the Enron scandal, so the behaviour of Evan Peterson in *A Story with a Health Warning* foreshadows more recent events. Peterson's lobbying activities bear a striking similarity to the egregious dealings of the former Conservative member of parliament, Owen Patterson, who was forced to resign his seat in the autumn of 2021 because of them.

MX Publishing

MX Publishing brings the best in new Sherlock Holmes novels, biographies, graphic novels and short story collections every month. With over 500 books it's the largest catalogue of new Sherlock Holmes books in the world.

We have over one hundred and fifty Holmes authors. The majority of our authors write new Holmes fiction - in all genres from very traditional pastiches through to modern novels, fantasy, crossover, children's books and humour.

In Holmes biography we have award winning historians including Alistair Duncan. Brian Pugh and Maureen Whittaker who have all won the Sherlock Holmes Book of The Year Award.

MX Publishing also has one of the largest communities of Holmes fans on Facebook and Twitter under @mxpublishing.

MX is a social enterprise that has raised over $100,000 for good causes including Happy Life Mission (Kenya), Undershaw School for children with learning disabilities (UK) and the WFP (World Food Programme).

www.mxpublishing.com

Also from MX Publishing

"Phil Growick's, 'The Secret Journal of Dr Watson', is an adventure which takes place in the latter part of Holmes and Watson's lives. They are entrusted by HM Government (although not officially) and the King no less to undertake a rescue mission to save the Romanovs, Russia's Royal family from a grisly end at the hand of the Bolsheviks. There is a wealth of detail in the story but not so much as would detract us from the enjoyment of the story. Espionage, counter-espionage, the ace of spies himself, double-agents, double-crossers...all these flit across the pages in a realistic and exciting way. All the characters are extremely well-drawn and Mr Growick, most importantly, does not falter with a very good ear for Holmesian dialogue indeed. Highly recommended. A five-star effort."
The Baker Street Society

www.mxpublishing.com

Also from MX Publishing

The Missing Authors Series

Sherlock Holmes and The Adventure of The Grinning Cat
Sherlock Holmes and The Nautilus Adventure
Sherlock Holmes and The Round Table Adventure

"Joseph Svec, III is brilliant in entwining two endearing and enduring classics of literature, blending the factual with the fantastical; the playful with the pensive; and the mischievous with the mysterious. We shall, all of us young and old, benefit with a cup of tea, a tranquil afternoon, and a copy of Sherlock Holmes, The Adventure of the Grinning Cat."
Amador County Holmes Hounds Sherlockian Society

www.mxpublishing.com

Also from MX Publishing

The American Literati Series

The Final Page of Baker Street
The Baron of Brede Place
Seventeen Minutes To Baker Street

"The really amazing thing about this book is the author's ability to call up the 'essence' of both the Baker Street 'digs' of Holmes and Watson as well as that of the 'mean streets' of Marlowe's Los Angeles. Although none of the action takes place in either place, Holmes and Watson share a sense of camaraderie and self-confidence in facing threats and problems that also pervades many of the later tales in the Canon. Following their conversations and banter is a return to Edwardian England and its certainties and hope for the future. This is definitely the world before The Great War."
Philip K Jones

Also from MX Publishing

The Detective and The Woman Series

   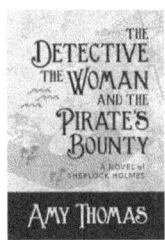

The Detective and The Woman

The Detective, The Woman and The Winking Tree

The Detective, The Woman and The Silent Hive

The Detective, The Woman and The Pirate's Bounty

"The book is entertaining, puzzling and a lot of fun. I believe the author has hit on the only type of long-term relationship possible for Sherlock Holmes and Irene Adler. The details of the narrative only add force to the romantic defects we expect in both of them and their growth and development are truly marvelous to watch. This is not a love story. Instead, it is a coming-of-age tale starring two of our favorite characters."

Philip K Jones

www.mxpublishing.com

Also from MX Publishing

The Sherlock Holmes and Enoch Hale Series

The Amateur Executioner
The Poisoned Penman
The Egyptian Curse

"The Amateur Executioner: Enoch Hale Meets Sherlock Holmes", the first collaboration between Dan Andriacco and Kieran McMullen, concerns the possibility of a Fenian attack in London. Hale, a native Bostonian, is a reporter for London's Central News Syndicate - where, in 1920, Horace Harker is still a familiar figure, though far from revered. "The Amateur Executioner" takes us into an ambiguous and murky world where right and wrong aren't always distinguishable. I look forward to reading more about Enoch Hale."
Sherlock Holmes Society of London

www.mxpublishing.com

Also from MX Publishing

When the papal apartments are burgled in 1901, Sherlock Holmes is summoned to Rome by Pope Leo XII. After learning from the pontiff that several priceless cameos that could prove compromising to the church, and perhaps determine the future of the newly unified Italy, have been stolen, Holmes is asked to recover them. In a parallel story, Michelangelo, the toast of Rome in 1501 after the unveiling of his Pieta, is commissioned by Pope Alexander VI, the last of the Borgia pontiffs, with creating the cameos that will bedevil Holmes and the papacy four centuries later. For fans of Conan Doyle's immortal detective, the game is always afoot. However, the great detective has never encountered an adversary quite like the one with whom he crosses swords in "The Vatican Cameos.."

"An extravagantly imagined and beautifully written Holmes story"
(**Lee Child**, NY Times Bestselling author, Jack Reacher series)

Also from MX Publishing

The Conan Doyle Notes (The Hunt For Jack The Ripper)
"Holmesians have long speculated on the fact that the Ripper murders aren't mentioned in the canon, though the obvious reason is undoubtedly the correct one: even if Conan Doyle had suspected the killer's identity he'd never have considered mentioning it in the context of a fictional entertainment. Ms Madsen's novel equates his silence with that of the dog in the night-time, assuming that Conan Doyle did know who the Ripper was but chose not to say – which, of course, implies that good old stand-by, the government cover-up. It seems unlikely to me that the Ripper was anyone famous or distinguished, but fiction is not fact, and "The Conan Doyle Notes" is a gripping tale, with an intelligent, courageous and very likable protagonist in DD McGil."
The Sherlock Holmes Society of London

www.mxpublishing.com